A

Pool of Swallows

Pool of Swallows

by Martin Cobalt

publishers since 1798

THOMAS NELSON INC.
NASHVILLE / NEW YORK

Library of Congress Cataloging in Publication Data

Cobalt, Martin.
    Pool of swallows.

    SUMMARY: A young farm boy tries to investigate some unnatural happenings, some of which are comic, some terrifying.
    [1. Mystery stories] I. Title.
PZ7.C6295Sw3   [Fic]   73–17033
ISBN 0–8407–6387–5

1

The Swallows were three pools of water below the cliff. Martin Babbacombe saw them shining duller than the grass of the field they were in as he came back from school. He had walked the two miles from Marret along the cliff top, and saved the bus fare. It was a fine afternoon now, but earlier there had been rain and the cliff path was muddy. As a walker comes from Marret he passes first behind the dunes, then climbs a field out of sight of the sea, comes along a hedge, and then is on the path. There is a fence between him and the edge, and the sea or the exposed sand lie below, nursed by the cliffs. Then the path turns from the sea, but still follows the cliffs. The cliff strikes out across dry land.

Looking down from the path one sees not the amphibious world of sand or the marine water, but green fields. There is a triangle of land sticking out into the water, about ten fields in size, hedged and neat, about forty-seven acres altogether. Here the land has settled in some prehistoric time, lower than the mainland behind it. An ancient fault, the geologists say, along this piece of coast where chalk and limestone meet. The lower land is lowest just below the cliffs, and rises

5

towards the sea, and has its own set of cliffs, a brownish patch if one looks from the sea, against the white of the land on either side.

In a place on the slope that allows it to overlook the sea is the farmhouse, Swallow Farm. Below the main cliff, in the lowest part, are the three Swallows. The biggest one is a hundred yards across, the next one two thirds of that, and the smallest one a mere puddle of about fifty feet. Water flows into them from the chalk but there is no obvious way for the water to get out again. In spite of that the level stays the same all the year round. Martin had once seen it changed.

Now he loitered on his way, doing nothing and thinking nothing, looking at the farmland below him and at the sea beyond. The sea went out misty into a middle distance and then stopped having anything that could be seen and stopped sending back any sunlight that was in the sky. Martin loitered instead of going home and being tied to the house, where nothing would happen to the rest of the day but its gradual extinction in farm doings. It would end, he knew, with his father asleep in his chair, and his sister would send him to bed and go on with her sewing or ironing, cross in herself with the tedium but unable to do anything about it. Like the level of water in the Swallows, there was never any change.

Martin leaned on the electricity pole at the cliff edge. It was the pole that held the supply line to the farm. To cling to its wire and slide would bring him down quickest to the wall of the house. Idly he contemplated a way of swinging round the posts in between him and the house. Ski-lifts did it, he thought, so perhaps it would be possible. The thought became so boring after a time that he wished he could forget it and think of something better, but nothing better came to mind.

He heard his father shout from below, not at him, but at the cows. He heard a field gate fall back open against its stop. A cow gave a shriek that sounded like mortal terror but was probably greedy anticipation of cake for tea, or whatever a cow thought the meal was that it took in the shippon when it was being milked.

Martin saw his father walk below him, ahead of the cows now by two fields, towards the shippon. The cows, slow to move at first, now began to wander from their pasture along the road. The road led past the Swallows, going between the two bigger ones. The cows followed, all nine of them. The leader stopped to sniff the water and suck up the edge of it. Martin was just above them all now and standing in the road himself, before it twisted to get down the gap in the main cliff. He thought that a well-thrown stone might liven up the cows and add something to the day. He was looking for a flint when he heard a bubbling noise.

At first he thought the noise came from some flow of water from the afternoon's rain, making its way across the chalk he stood on. He could not focus the sound near to himself at all, and walked from side to side of the white, sticky road to find what it was. When he came to the cliff edge once more he heard the noise more clearly, and knew that it came from below.

There was a boiling and a seething in the Swallows. The water was moving and swirling. The cows looked at it, some in the big Swallow and some in the smaller one. Martin saw them backing away from either Swallow, on to the road, and wondered why, and what wind blew down there that did not blow up on the still cliff.

He saw the waters of the Swallows rise. They did not rise quite in silence, because there was still that forcing bubbling noise. They rose fast, however, and covered the road. The cows stood in water. They looked as idly at it as Martin had looked at the sea not long before. The water, Martin saw, had risen calm. He could see the cows reflected in it, the pink of udders and the white of bellies. Then there was no reflection any more, because the water was higher than udders and bellies. Now there was splashing, and the water still came up, spreading so that there was one Swallow now, and one long lake instead of three small ponds. Martin saw, without quite watching, that his father had reached the shippon and was turning to shout for the cows again. He saw his father see him and wave, which was an order to get down off the cliff and hurry them cows on, you idle ninny.

No words came that Martin heard. The splashing in the Swallows was from the cows. They were having to swim, and they were startled. Martin took a step forward, and then withdrew it. There was nothing he could do, either in action or thought, and nothing he could take in except with his eyes. His knees no longer held him up, and he knelt in the road. Flints dug at his skin and the knobs of his knees but he did not feel that sudden agony.

The cows seemed to be swimming in a circle, and to have spread out of a herd into a line. At first Martin thought that was a better thing happening, until he saw, with a new horror at something so unnatural, that two of them were swimming backwards.

Now he knew all moderation and sense had gone out of the world. He saw the gyrations of the beasts and knew they were all circling the big Swallow. He saw that the water was spinning and falling, but not evenly. The middle of the Swallow was the lowest part, and there there was a round brown lazing eye, it seemed, looking back at him. Round the rim of this eye the nine cows span, no longer appearing to swim the right or the wrong way, but themselves spinning and being turned over and over, so that he saw heads and horns and legs and bellies and udders as if a model farmyard were being stirred in a bucket.

One by one the creatures were pulled out of the rim and went down into the central eye. Nine times the central eye winked at Martin, before gazing unblinkingly at him. Then it was no longer there. The iris contracted, the level rose, the Swallow was at its own restful height. There was no more disturbance.

Mr Babbacombe came down from the shippon himself, since shouting for the cows had not brought them, and shouting at Martin had not moved him to do anything. He came all the way to the Swallows, looked round, seemed to see nothing amiss, and went on beyond them, supposing that he had not left the gate open, or that some wayward cow had rubbed against it and shut the herd the wrong side.

He came back in his slow way and went right up to the shippon, and looked in. Then he retraced his steps to the Swallows and stood beside the big one, and called again.

Martin got up from his knees. He wanted to shout down with some message, but he did not know the purpose of the message or what it could say. And he was wondering how he had stayed alive himself and whether he had been meant to. It would have been easier to go as the cows had gone.

He remembered that other time clearly, and grew frightened and angry at the memory. The fright was new, but the anger was old. He wondered when it had happened. He thought it must have been about seven years ago ... Seven seemed to him to be a reasonable guess, as well as being somehow scriptural. Pharaoh's kine had been in a river, or water of some sort, he remembered, and they were concerned with seven years. Seven years ago he would have been six years old. He had been coming along the road alone, perhaps following Jane at a long distance. He knew he was on the way to the top fields, above the main cliff, because it was there that he had been scolded unfairly, because of not being able to explain. He thought something like that would happen again; some things could not be explained.

He had been beside the Swallows, or between the two big ones, just as the cows had been. He remembered what he had done then that made it impossible to explain. He had pulled up the leg of his shorts and peed a yellow tinkle into the middle-sized Swallow; not into the big one, because that would have been cheek, but into the middle one.

Straight away the waters had risen at him, swift and cold about his ankles, tingling against his knees. He had watched fascinated, but not alarmed, pulling at his shorts to keep them from the water, and giggling gently at the tickling feeling. He had pulled in vain. The water had come up, darkened the hem of his trousers, retreated down to his knees, come up and kissed him cold between the legs, hugged him damp about his waist, and then dropped away, leaving his clothes stuck to him and making him feel heavier, because when the water was highest it had lifted and lightened him without taking him from the ground.

He had not been able to tell Jane what had happened, and what he did say she did not credit. She had pulled his clothes from him, slapped his cold wet rump, and made him walk down to the house naked, and a nettle had got up against him and rashed his belly.

That was bad enough then, because of the injustice.

Jane thought he had walked into the Swallow after wetting his shorts, to hide the fact. Martin had thought then and thought now that he was much too old for that to have happened. Then he remembered that Jane was only his own present age when it happened, and he was able to forgive her. In any case the injustice of it, even the physical matter of the slap and the nettle, seemed to matter very little now, when he thought that he might have been taken as the cows had been taken, stirred and struggling, threshing in the fast pool and then absorbed into the gaze of that eye.

He tried to walk now, but his legs would not go with him. They refused again to hold him, and this time he sank down into a sitting position by the road. The sun flicked a ray of light at him, and he felt the heat on his skin. The heat turned dank and chill, as if water were once more rising at him. The sky came very close and then turned black, and his head went pouring down a whirlpool through his eyes, sky and time and land and sea turning to darkness and oblivion.

He was trembling and feeling sick. Time had gone by, he knew, but not how much. The memory of the cows was distinct now, and a little distant. Their vanishing was no longer a present thing, but a past event. He wondered if he had dreamed it, with that aching tight small head he had. He sat up, wondering why he had been lying down, and the sky blinked black until he kept still and moved his head slowly with his eyes shut. He opened them and found he was looking out over the Swallows, and there was the fat smelly figure of his father, looking up towards him and shouting.

Martin was not yet ready to listen to anything more than the sea-sounds in his ears. He kept his head still and the sea-sounds began to pour out of his left ear, and that became clearer. But then the right ear began to fill up, and the sound rose higher and higher, until he was seeing the sound as well as hearing it, and tasting it, and the sky was the colour of the sound.

The next waking was different. He was being whirled round and round in some enormous Swallow, but in a metal box. He wanted to see who was in all the other metal boxes, and he could smell the oil, he was a tinned fish. They put sacks in the tins, and he was glad.

He woke again, and he was by the kitchen fire, spread out on a big chair, and that was home. Jane and his father were looking at him. Jane was stirring the teapot with one hand and feeling Martin's head with the other.

'How be, then?' said his father.

'Fainty-like still, then?' said Jane. 'Would you like a cup of tea, Martin?'

'Yes,' said Martin. 'I'm not faint any more.'

'You sure, like?' said Jane. 'Dad found you to the cliff-top, why, you might have rolled over, and he brought you on in the tractor box. You haven't broken any bones, or nothing like that, have you, Martin?'

'Don't drawl on so,' said Martin. 'You sound like an old woman.'

'Yes, I do do that,' said Jane. 'I suppose you must be to rights, if you be picking on me like that.'

'Fair bound to be,' said Mr Babbacombe. 'I'll get on out then and milk they cows. They'll be waiting.' He stumped off through the kitchen door. But after he had filled the doorway with his body and then lessened the eclipse by going into the yard a little way, he came back, darkening again. 'Martin, boy,' he said. 'I be going to milk them, surely, but where in God's name are the buggers?'

2

Sergeant Lowes leaned back in his chair, belched a bacony belch, tasting his breakfast again as it went through his nose, and waited for someone to come in for him to speak to. While he waited he looked from the Police Station window at the town of Marret with the sea beyond it. The weather was too warm, he thought, but the sunshine picked the town out brightly and the mist across the sea made a background. Two fishing boats were going out of the harbour with bare masts. There was no wind at all, and they were motoring out.

Constable Zeal came in. 'Thundery, Sergeant,' he said.

'You're right, boy,' said Sergeant Lowes. 'Have you ever thought, lad, that there's six thousand people out there.'

'Approximately,' said Constable Zeal. 'They come and go a bit.'

'Don't think approximate,' said Sergeant Lowes. 'Two and two make an exact four each time. But you're right if you mean the six thousand are approximately there. But call it six thousand exactly, and think what would

13

happen if one per cent of them, that's one in a hundred ...'

'Sixty,' said Constable Zeal. 'To the nearest whole person.'

'It's always whole people,' said Sergeant Lowes, 'unless someone's been careless with an axe. But that's what I'm thinking about. If sixty people suddenly decided to commit serious crimes all at once, separately, we'd be hard up to catch them all.'

'It's possible that we might be among the sixty,' said Constable Zeal. 'You or me or one of the others.'

'That'd help,' said Sergeant Lowes. 'Anyway, that's one example, one per cent. But what if it was two per cent, more than a hundred criminals with their axes and parts of people buried in the cellar. And if you can have two per cent why not ten. We might have six hundred wild criminals in our midst now, out there pouring poison into their husbands' coffee, holding up both banks, pushing valuable dogs down wells, actively engaged in piracy in the harbour, driving away cars without the owners' consent, parking on double yellow lines and selling game without a licence.'

'They'd be tripping over each other,' said Constable Zeal. 'About how many bodies do you expect, and what arrangements should we make?'

'I wish you would make conversation sometimes like a human,' said Sergeant Lowes. 'Or have you a sense of humour I don't understand? It's serious, think of all those dairymen adulterating the milk with water.'

'Or vodka,' said Constable Zeal.

'That's more like it,' said Sergeant Lowes. 'Go out and buy a couple of pints.'

Constable Zeal smiled. 'I have already done that,' he said. 'But purely as a householder and domestic man. Our milkman did not come this morning.'

14

Constable Zeal went to his place behind the counter in the station office. Sergeant Lowes contracted his stomach and waited for another belch, but it was not time for one yet. He went on with his typing. What would happen, truly, he wondered, if three per cent, or a hundred and eighty, citizens decided on lives of crime?

Half an hour later Constable Zeal came in with a cup of tea.

'Crime wave's a bit slow starting,' he said. 'But there's a funny tale come in from along the coast.'

'Smuggling,' said Sergeant Lowes. 'I hadn't thought of that, but its obvious, isn't it, all those fishing boats?'

'Just a bit of gossip,' said Constable Zeal. 'Explains why I had no milk this morning.'

'Go on,' said Sergeant Lowes. 'Gossip's one, and one is half of two, and two two's are four and that's as far as you need add.'

'Babbacombe,' said Constable Zeal.

'I can tell you,' said Sergeant Lowes. 'Drunk and disorderly. But not in this town. Where did he do it and what's the damage?'

'That's the man,' said Constable Zeal. 'Black Babbacombe of Swallow Farm.'

'He can swallow,' said Sergeant Lowes. 'But he's behaved himself for a long time now. That daughter of his, she doesn't say much but she's tightened him down a turn or so. So he's started coming home with the milk, as you might say, once more, has he?'

'You're making too much of it,' said Constable Zeal.

'We're a long way off one per cent,' said Sergeant Lowes. 'That's all.'

'Now, the thing about Black Babbacombe is that he didn't come home with the milk last night,' said Constable Zeal. 'Or that's the story. He went out to milk

15

at the usual time, but there wasn't any milk to be got.'

'I remember when I was a lad,' said Sergeant Lowes, 'there was an old woman in the village and they reckoned she was a witch and she'd do such things as dry the cows up so that they have no milk or calved wrong, or the wind got in the crops or the chimney smoked. Stuff like that.'

'Bad enough,' said Constable Zeal. 'And there's still a law against witchcraft. But you'd never catch a real witch, she'd turn you into a toad promptly.'

'You'd still have powers of arrest,' said Sergeant Lowes. 'You remember that, lad.'

'I'll go on about Black Babbacombe,' said Constable Zeal. 'It wasn't just milk he was without, but all his cows. It seems he saw them in the field, opened the gate for them, went to the shippon, and, you know, they'd walk along to him while he got ready for them. But yesterday they didn't come.'

'Go on,' said Sergeant Lowes.

'Babbacombe's lad saw what happened, he says,' said Constable Zeal. 'Those ponds called the Swallows, the cows had to pass by them. The water rose up and sucked all the cows in and down and seemingly drowned the lot.'

'Gossip,' said Sergeant Lowes. 'That's not a crime wave, it's a tidal wave.'

'It's an unlikely story,' said Constable Zeal.

'That's true,' said Sergeant Lowes. 'But it's only a story, and I don't reckon much of it either. I mean, I'd think better of it as an explanation for losing my cows if those ponds hadn't got a funny name already. There's been tales about them for years. I wonder if Black Babbacombe's going to claim insurance on a herd of cows he's sold somewhere else. Never mind about the tale of the Swallows. The missing cows are the impor-

16

tant thing. You get along there and get the story from Black's own lips, and that's one out of two, and see if you can't get the other one to make two, and find out that a cattle wagon went that way some time recently, and see whether he didn't sell them a month ago and has bought milk ever since to hand on to supply the dairy. You'll find folk who've seen the cows, or not seen them. And don't take any notice of tales about herds of cows being swallowed up. I'll bet this is an ordinary fraud, and if we look we'll catch him, and the sooner we look the better because there'll be an insurance claim, and if he makes an insurance claim for something he's sold he'll be in trouble, so we want to stop him doing that. So you find out about it all and tell him to behave himself, the silly old fool, disgracing his family like that.'

*   *   *

Martin Babbacombe had stopped thinking with any sort of clarity about the previous day's events. Most of them he thought of not at all, the ordinary sequence of going to school and what went on there and returning home. There was a clear moment he dared think on, when he was by the electricity pole and the day was its drab self. Beyond that he did not care to remember in detail. The taking of the cattle lay like a fist through the page of the day, where nothing could be read. Mostly there was now in mind the long margin of the evening when his father had walked into every field, shouting for the cows, and then brought his search smaller and smaller until it lay along the track the cows must have taken, and at last centred on the Swallows without any word from Martin.

Martin had heard the search from the kitchen. Jane had gone on with preparations for tea, but more and more slowly. At last even she had stopped, when Mr Babbacombe's cries in the field became more desperate and he came to the door and moaned at them understanding nothing and unable to say anything. Jane had gone out with her hands under her apron and stood by the gate.

'I don't know what to do,' she had said. 'What shall I do, Martin? What's happened to the cows, boy?'

Martin swallowed when he had heard that, and had not been able to speak about it. His father had come in at last and sat at the table for tea. Instead of eating he had drunk three bottles of beer and grown more silent, and then gone out again and walked the fields. He had come in at last and said the curse was on them, and it was the end of the farm; they had been accursed since they came there. Then he had gone out, returning very noisily at a late hour and leaving the kitchen door open. His own dog Robot had bitten him on the leg in the morning. Then Martin had left the house and gone to school. Jane had said she would go shopping for most of the day. While Martin walked with Jane up the road he told her what he had seen the afternoon before. They had stood in the road and looked at the three innocent pools below.

'Well,' Jane had said, 'I don't know that I rightly believe it, Martin. It doesn't sound credible to me, like.'

She had considered the report all the way to the bus, and when it came she had let Martin go and turned back herself to the farm, because, she said, somebody had to tell him what had happened, or he'd be running about crazy the rest of his days.

At school there was a story about lost cows. The details were not known to anyone then, but it was supposed that Black Babbacombe had done something with the cows and was about to astonish the country or make a lot of money. Opinion was that this time he would be caught. Martin did not mind that his father was called Black Babbacombe by everyone, and that he was supposed to be a villain of no particular attainment but great repute. Sometimes Martin had tried to look at his father through the eyes of his schoolmates, to see whether in this dull man on a dull farm there could be a sparkling original villain. There never was. He only saw a bad-tempered fattish man who got drunk every few weeks and spent the rest of the time working on the farm or asleep in a chair. There could be nobody less noticeable, Martin thought. How could any reputation accrue to such a man?

Before dinner time there was more evidence of what had happened yesterday. Milk for the school came nearly directly from Swallow Farm. Today there was no milk, or only a small part of the usual delivery. News came quickly through the kitchen about what had happened, and then questions came quickly in turn to Martin.

'Tell us *all* about it, *at* once,' said Stinking Tom and Pewter, taking him away to the cupboard in the gym.

'*In* words,' said Pewter, who had very little shine, or even stink, of his own.

Martin was unwilling to think of what had happened, but even more unwilling to undergo Stinking Tom's tortures. He told them briefly what he had seen. Stinking Tom let him go and Pewter took away his not-very-formidable paws.

'We think, blow that for a yarn,' said Tom. 'Don't we, Pewter?'

'*Don't* we,' said Pewter. 'Do *better*, Babby.'

'Cows don't *do* that sort of thing,' said Stinking Tom.

'They didn't,' said Martin. 'It was done to them.'

'Cobblers,' said Stinking Tom, exhaling an odour of fish and departing. Pewter waved a flabby lizard hand and followed.

*　　*　　*

The town was not averse to the news. Without feeling it necessary to wonder whether it was true or not, the gossips handed it on. By the end of the day there were three versions of what had happened. One approximated to the truth, but all the members of the family had been taken as well and somebody's cousin had seen it happen. Another had the maddened and starved herd hurl itself from the cliff above desperate with thirst, to drown in the Swallows. The third had a small landslide, a pointing hand, and the voice of God from a cloud saying that so would sinners be punished, with no regard for the fact that cows have little capability for sin and were insured in any case. All versions agreed that the wickedness of Black Babbacombe was at the root of it all, and it was time such a villain met some justice better than any this world could provide.

There were other opinions, though, that considered what was in the stories, and were expressed by those who had long memories and had lived nearby for a long time.

'I remember when I was a boy,' said one old fisherman, now tied to the land but casting his line from the end of the jetty, 'that they had a boat up there, little brown row-boat from the harbour here, for the childer to go about the Swallow. That little boat was one day found smashed up, as if a demon done it, on the edge of those Swallows. Smashed up, and I saw it myself. That's a bad place, there, if such can happen in a night, smashed and crushed like it was trod on or been between a big boat and the jetty here. That whole place up there is unlucky, that whole place. Maybe it suits Black Babbacombe, but it wouldn't suit me.'

3

The headquarters of the Clandestine Insurance Company were in London; the local office that served Marret was in the County Town. What might otherwise have been a small flat smelling of babies and baked beans and inhabited by students who raised one and ate the other was instead the daily home of Miss Slingsby, who smelt, Mr Dawson said, of violets; she however maintained that the scent was Joyeuse, thank you, Mr Dawson. She would come in first in the morning, dismiss the vapours of floor polish and replace it with ones that were partly Joyeuse and partly tired mineral oil from the filing cabinets. Sometimes she would bring a flower that was no longer wanted at home, insure its life with water and aspirin and wait until it died to collect the petals. Mr Dawson would come in a little later than Miss Slingsby and read the letters. This was a ritual conducted with closed eyes and unopened envelopes, and in her most critical moments Miss Slingsby would call the process sleep. Mr Dawson said that he had never in fact observed himself asleep. But Miss Slingsby thought he knew, the sly one. She would take her large-sided face back to the typewriter and become busy.

This morning Mr Dawson came in as usual, took the

letters, and ambled into his room. Miss Slingsby heard the chair creak. She occupied herself with the typing of an inventory. The day was normal for all of them: Mr Dawson prepared for the day, Miss Slingsby put her mind into the automatic gear that let her get on with her thoughts while her fingers moved in obedience to her eyes, which read a page written by Mr David Hayman, the assistant. The typewriter typed the inventory as it had typed hundreds before. A fly in the window, tiring of the insurance business, buzzed against the glass. No one inside heard it. No one outside could see it.

The office door opened and David Hayman came in. He said nothing, but indicated Mr Dawson's office with his head. Miss Slingsby said nothing back, but, looking at Mr Hayman, closed her eyes for a brief moment, and smiled.

The telephone rang. The fly in the window buzzed as loudly as it could, as if there were some competition between it and the black machine. Miss Slingsby dropped the word she was typing and lifted the phone. Mr Hayman went to the window and put a finger on the fly until it stopped buzzing. Then he put it between his fingers and held it without crushing it.

'Clandestine,' said Miss Slingsby. Then she sat wooden, like a once-painted but now fading Indian, while the telephone, David supposed, spoke to her. As it went on speaking she covered the mouthpiece and said with her mouth in the automatic way that she would have typed with her fingers, 'Babbacombe, Swallow Farm, Marret, insurance on cows. Yes, Mr Babbacombe.'

David put the fly in a desk drawer for the time being, since he had not had time to open the window and expel it. He went to the sour-smelling filing cabinets and looked under the B's until he found Babbacombe, and handed the folder to Miss Slingsby. She waved it back to him, and said into the telephone, 'I'll see whether our Mr Hayman can speak to you, Sir, if you'll hold the line a moment.'

'Let me read the record first,' said David. 'There isn't much here. Let's see, farm stock. What's his story, young Slingsby?'

'He's lost all his cows,' said Miss Slingsby. 'He's very excited about it.'

'Let them alone, And they'll come home, Leaving their tails behind them,' said David. 'But that's lambs, isn't it? All his cows, did you say?'

'He said,' said Miss Slingsby. 'He wants us to pay up. Are we covered?'

'Tell him you're checking his cover,' said David. 'Ask him how many cows it was.'

Miss Slingsby asked, and reported nine cows.

'We'll have to look into that,' said David. 'But I won't speak to him now. Put him through to Mr Dawson, and I'll take the folder in, and then I'll go down to where-is-it and look around.'

'Marret,' said Miss Slingsby. 'Mr Dawson, Mr Hayman is just coming in with a question about a client I have on the line now.'

Mr Dawson grunted into the telephone, and gave a sort of shout through the closed door. David went in to the further office.

'Quite right,' said Mr Dawson, when he heard an outline. 'We can't make any statement whatever until it has been looked into. There may be more than a thousand pounds involved here, though I very much doubt it. You go down, David, and look into it.' Then he picked up the telephone and spoke to Mr Babbacombe.

'Really?' he said. 'How extraordinary, my goodness.'
He waved to David to get on to another telephone and
listen, but by the time he had got into the other office
and picked it up the extraordinary part seemed to be
over, and Mr Babbacombe was only asking how soon
he would have his money.

'What do you think, David?' said Mr Dawson. 'You'd
better go on down there and look into it. I don't like it
at all, a very unlikely tale, the cat hasn't a longer one.'

But then two clients came in to the outer office, and
the telephone rang again, and there was no time for
Mr Dawson to say more. 'Go and find out,' he said.
'Don't start with any notions of your own. Go on, take
the file with you.'

David took that file, and other papers he would need
during the day, and went out to his car. He had other
calls to make as he went, and it was late afternoon
before he came to Marret.

It was obvious that the farm would not be in the
middle of the town, but all the same that was where he
went first. For one thing the farm could not be far off,
and must lie east or west or north, because of the coast.
For another he did not want to approach without finding out something of the place. He parked the car by
the harbour and got out, looking to see who might be
a local inhabitant. He thought it might be a mistake to
come right down here, because those who were not
visitors seemed to be fishermen and sailors, and sailors
would not know about farms.

He was about to walk up into the town when he
heard the name Babbacombe on the lips of a very old
fisherman, linked with the words Swallow Farm. The
ancient fisherman was carrying a small unhealthy fish
that looked slimy.

25

'Fishing, then, Dad?' said David, walking alongside the old man.

'No, I wouldn't like to say that,' said the old man. 'This specimen I picked up at the water's edge and I'm going to drop him in the litter bin yonder. I never caught a thing today, but that's all right, for I don't want a thing, I just do it for the habit, and it's something to do at my age and I can talk too at the same time. But just now I be going to my tea.'

'I heard you speak about Babbacombe at Swallow Farm,' said David. 'Didn't I?'

'You might,' said the old man, pausing by a litter bin. He lifted the fish high and released it. It fell into the bin and straight out through the bottom again and lay in the gutter. The old man did not notice. David looked the other way. 'You might,' said the old man again. 'They get mentioned this day. Now, I mind when I was a boy they had this little brown row-boat up there, up in them Swallows for the childer, but you'm bound to have heard about that, so I won't say no more.'

'No, I haven't heard,' said David. 'And I want to know where Swallow Farm is?'

'Black Babbacombe's, eh, you want to know where that's to? I can show you that. Now, see along there, that headland to the east?'

David was puzzled by this. The old man was pointing, presumably in an easterly direction, but immediately to the east, if that was the right way, there was a high wall, since David and the old man had left the open place of the harbour and were in a street.

'Yes,' he said, not very enthusiastically.

'You can just see along the side where the roof to the farm is,' said the old man. 'There's two big hedges run up to it and you can see the light in the window.'

'Yes, I see it,' said David, wondering what defect of

26

vision the old man had that let him see through walls to lights that would not be alight at this time of day.

'You young fool,' said the old man. 'You can't see un from here. You'll have to go back to where we was to afore we set off for here. Near where I dropped that fish on the floor, that's a right one for the council, they should get a bottom in those baskets. I can't see through a stone wall, and if you can, young man, go and see through another one; that there's the Ladies.'

'You've been very helpful,' said David, turning round and walking away. Black Babbacombe? he thought. That sounds more like a pirate's name than a farmer's. Then he came back to where he had met the fisherman, and looked to the east. He could see now what he had been told to see. If he had wanted to go there by boat he would have been admirably guided, but he had little indication of the right road. He asked again at a shop and had the route drawn for him on a paper bag, and welcome, they told him. He heard too that something had come and killed all the cows in the night and half-eaten bodies strewed the whole farm. The shop itself did not believe that all the family had been eaten too, it would have been on telly by now, and the shop watched telly most nights. But whatever it was, as an old inhabitant, the shop knew the Babbacombes had never been popular, and Black Babbacombe's mother had been a witch, that was well known, and used to get things up out of the water. Horrible things. And welcome again. You'll be a relative?

'No, just curious,' said David, and indeed he was.

A reporter, that's it, said the shop, you're welcome, our name's on the bag.

David went to a telephone and rang the office and asked Miss Slingsby for the full and true history of Mr Babbacombe's cows and anything else she knew. She did not know the full and true history, only that the cows were lost, and Mr Babbacombe hadn't said dead. He had used a great many unfamiliar words, but none of them meant dead, only lost. Mr Dawson knew the whole story but he had left the office early. David said he would do his best with what he had ... He considered going to the Police Station and asking there, but decided against that, because it was unlikely that he would be told anything, and very often a client did not like to think that he had asked the police for any help at all, if there was no question of robbery. Though of course it was possible that the cows had been stolen, even if the feeling of the shop was that something dramatic and violent had happened.

He took the shop's directions and left the town. He wanted the third turn to the right. Before he got to that he saw a man doing some agricultural thing to a hedge with a hooked tool, and stopped to pass the time of day with him.

'You'll not be Mr Babbacombe, will you?' he asked.

'I shouldn't hardly think so,' said the man, bringing down the hooked and bladed implement and springing it quivering into a tree stump. He look at David enquiringly.

'I don't want to go past the turning,' said David. The man came nearer the car and looked in.

'Erfishel,' he said. 'I can tell. Ministry, or County Council, or something of the sort. Erfishel.'

'Insurance,' said David. 'More use, eh?'

'I work for the County Council myself,' said the man. 'Name of Hagblow. Swallow's the next turn-off, shouldn't wonder if the gate wasn't closed, like. A sorry affair down there, I hear, eh?'

'I heard something,' said David.

'I knew they was for it,' said Mr Hagblow. 'I knew

it this spring when the rooks took and left the trees there and never built a scrap of a nest, they're knowing birds. And never a gull on the cliffs, you can't say they don't know, for they do. They should have left afore. Seagulls ain't nothing, but rooks is luck, I wouldn't care to be abandoned by a rook, that I wouldn't.'

'I've never been adopted by one,' said David.

'Never ... Haw,' said Mr Hagblow. 'That's good, never being adopted by a rook, I should think not, you'm thinking of storks, man.'

'Well, thanks for your help, Mr Hagblow,' said David, and drove on.

The gate was closed when he came to it. He opened it and drove towards the sea. After the second gate he met someone else. It was a policeman in a glistening uniform. The policeman waved him down.

'Excuse me, Sir,' said the policeman. 'I'm Constable Zeal of Marret, but speaking as a civilian I might advise you to go no farther. Mr Babbacombe is in an excited state, and he has just thrown me in one his ponds.'

David explained who he was and the purpose of his visit. Constable Zeal suggested he should wait nearby in case Mr Babbacombe was again dissatisfied, but David thought he would be able to manage alone. The Constable walked on, wheeling a wet moped.

The road ran apparently over the edge of the cliff. David went forward carefully and picked his way down when he saw how the land really lay. The corner was a tight one for the car, and he negotiated it slowly. Then stopped. Coming up the road towards him was an army of small animals, all of them in a hurry and all of them tolling up the slope. At the head loped two dogs, and to one side five cats, slinking with ears back and a shamefaced look. Behind the dogs jigged four hares and a number of rabbits who were continually stamping on the road and looking insane. After the rabbits was a bevy of hedgehogs, and following them eight grey squirrels, and rustling behind them a rope of snakes, and at the back another rope of a thicker kind that was made of weasels and stoats. Farther down the road, coming independently, were two large badgers and two small ones. Moving close by the road in the grass were little migrant colonies of mice and shrews. David stopped the car engine and waited. The stream of animals passed him by almost in silence, and went on up the slope and over the top of the cliff. He waited until they had gone, and then took some notice of what they had done. They had come from the low-lying land, and, if, like rooks, they knew something, then David was going to be wary like them. He backed the car to the top of the cliff, and walked down, past the pools of water, past the shippon, and to the farm.

4

Pewter went off among the houses, but Stinking Tom followed Martin homewards. The cliff path was not wide enough for two to walk side by side, so someone had to follow, and Martin only unwillingly accepted Stinking Tom's company. At one time he hoped Tom was about to give up and go home, and at another he thought how possible it would be to push him over the cliff. Stinking Tom elaborated reasons as they went, reasons for wanting to lose nine cows. His sing-song voice trailed Martin until he became used to it and it was no more than a following breeze would have been. Cow-pox was one of his theories, and another was that they had 'dried up' and presumably shrivelled to neat little bundles that could be stacked in a hiding place until they had been paid for and replaced. The bodies would then be fossilized or sunk in the sea or sold to a 'manufacturer'. Martin knew that Stinking Tom thought manufacturing was the making of things called manufactures. It is, of course, but Tom thought that all manufacturing towns made one article all the time, a manufacture, and he had not felt the need to imagine what a manufacture could be like. He had a vague theory that manufacturers were wicked, and another that Black Babbacombe was wicked, so the two hung together quite well in his mind. Or, he conjectured, the cows had been used in witchcraft, along with the eye of newt and things like that. It was well known, he said, that Martin's grandmother had been a witch and had been burnt for it.

Martin had difficulty arguing about that, though it was not strictly true. His grandfather and father had attempted a home cremation after the old lady, and she had been very old, was dead. They had been trying to save money, and they had almost succeeded. The undertaker had known what they intended to do and instead of sending the old lady's body back to Swallow Farm in the coffin he had sent clothes and stones of about the same weight. The two men had lit a huge funeral pyre with the coffin on it and waited to see what happened. Nothing had happened. The fire had burnt all night and nothing was left. In the morning the undertaker had sent round a black car and taken the party off to the proper crematorium. Martin could just remember something about the affair. Shortly after it his mother had gone away too, and that meant more black cars. Black cars by the farm smelt of doom to him.

He did not trouble to explain to Tom about his grandmother. Tom went from dried up cows to a disease called continuous aversion, he said, in which cows don't like anything and die of dislike.

'The truth is,' said Martin, at last, when they had come to the road down the cliff and were about to stand where he had stood the day before, 'the truth is that they were turned into toads and they hobbled away and we let them go because nobody drinks toad milk these days.'

Then there was a curious noise down below. Martin stepped forward, glad this time to have a witness, even Stinking Tom, if the Swallows were going to perform again. The noise came from a moped and its rider, who were trying to hasten away from an angry round figure who was chasing them with a dung fork. The moped would start its engine in bursts and then expire before the rhythm caught and the moped would stop with the rider half on it. Each time it happened the dung fork would come nearer. At last it happened that was bound to happen: the fork did not stay in Black Babbacombe's hand. It left it and went through the spokes of the back wheel of the moped, stopping it abruptly so that the newly mounted rider fell off and the machine fell over.

Black Babbacombe seized the rider first, picked him up, and hurled him into the biggest of the Swallows. He landed spreadeagled like a toad, underlining what Martin had just told Stinking Tom. The moped followed, and lay in the shallows with its tyres spinning slowly and dabbling the water with their tread.

'That's a bobby,' said Stinking Tom. Mr Babbacombe had found the policeman's cap and thrown it after him. 'That's one of our town bobbies.'

'Watch him change colour. He'll be a toad in a minute right enough,' said Martin.

'Get out, he never will,' said Stinking Tom. He was not. He floundered until the bottom was flat enough to stand on, and then he walked out of the water and pulled at the cuffs of his tunic, as if that would help dry him. He waded in again and pulled up the moped, getting his cuffs wet once more.

'Black Babbacombe's for it now,' said Stinking Tom. 'Eh?'

'I didn't see it, did I?' said Martin. 'I was looking

sea. Thinking about toads.'

king Tom thought about that, or toads, for a
nd then smiled. 'I get you,' he said. 'We'll go
wn.'

They walked down the road, talking of other things.
Martin was wondering chiefly why the dog Robot was
frantically and single-mindedly pulling himself out of
his collar, every now and then stopping to draw a breath
that croaked in his lungs as if they would burst.

The police constable was standing beside the moped
when they reached him, kicking it to start it. Nothing
was happening except that each time a few drops of
water would spurt from the exhaust pipe.

'Have you two boys just come down the road?' said
the constable.

'Yes,' said Martin. 'I've just come back from school.'

'I have just been thrown into that piece of water,'
said the constable. 'I wish to prefer a charge against
the person who threw me in. Did either of you two
witness the incident?'

'I've been looking at the sea,' said Martin. That was
not totally a lie, but he was prepared to lie all the time
if he had to.

'I saw it all,' said Stinking Tom.

'You didn't,' said Martin.

'I did,' said Tom. 'You were riding along, mister,
and you went round the corner too fast, easy to see that,
it was. You skidded, like, and went arse-on-top into
the water, and your bike ran after you. You've broken
that, I reckon, cracked the cylinder, I shouldn't
wonder.'

'Is that what you saw?' said the constable.

'Surely,' said Stinking Tom. 'No more than that. Mr
Babbacombe, he went for a rope to drag 'ee out.'

'And a towel. To dry on,' said Martin. 'Surely.'

34

'Is that the case, is that the attitude?' said Constable Zeal. 'Well, I'll report the matter, and if you get called as witness then you'll have to take the oath and speak the truth.'

He did not stay to speak any more because Mr Babbacombe came out from behind the shippon riding the tractor backwards, so that what came towards the constable was the flowery wire sculpture of a hay-tedder, four yellow raised wheels geared to the axle below and coming along the road like a dragon.

The constable leaned on his handlebars and addressed himself to the hill. As soon as he moved the tractor stopped, and stood watching. The constable did not stand, but went on pushing his way up the slope. The dog Robot pulled his head free of his collar, scratched at a bleeding ear, and went off on some errand of his own. The policeman went out of sight. The tractor went forward again to its place behind the shippon, and Mr Babbacombe walked off into the fields beyond the farm.

'Then I'm off too,' said Stinking Tom. 'I reckon you'll all be locked up before so long. But I saw him ride into the water, I shan't change that ...'

'See you then,' said Martin, suddenly reluctant now to let even Stinking Tom go away, now that the alternative was only the unexpectedly violent but still very dull patch of land and life called home.

'Right enough,' said Stinking Tom. He turned to go, but stopped where he was in the road. 'O God, my God,' he said, 'what's this now. It is witchcraft, he's been changing people, look, Babbacombe.'

Seven snakes were coming along the road. Usually Martin would have thought them gliding and lovely, but they had so much compound determination expressed in the way they came on and came on without

35

turning aside, that he felt alarmed. The snakes were not alone. In the grass beside the road there was a running and a chattering and a moving, of mice disturbing the grass and not showing, and rats leaping and looking, and all going the same way as the snakes.

Then Robot came running towards them, his mouth bleeding, where he had chewed through the collars of the other dogs and let them loose. They were following the snakes and mice, and they passed them without turning to look at them, and came on in front, passing Martin and Stinking Tom.

Stinking Tom, however, did not wait for snakes, or for the other animals that were coming on to the road now: cats oblivious of the mice, hedgehogs careless of the light, lizards twitching in the sun, squirrels out of their trees. Tom went ahead of them all, and strode past the dogs and up the slope of the road where it climbed the cliff. Martin stood away from the road and watched the procession go by. Now, he thought, doom was not shown merely by the presence of black cars. There must be something remarkable in the place to drive all these creatures away like that, fearless of one another, intent, all in one direction. Was this the witchcraft that Stinking Tom said it was that somehow, he knew, belonged to this place and this farm? What had yesterday to do with today?

He heard Jane singing in the house, and then stop singing in the middle of a note, and three doors slam in a windless day. He went in, because it was tea time, and found the house full of coal smoke from the fire. And that, he knew, was proof of witchcraft.

* * *

There was a whistling noise coming from the farm-house as David approached it. There seemed to be no other noise here at all; no birds, no farm creatures, no dogs. David thought he must have seen them all leave. But there were people here: one farmer who threw men into ponds was enough for the mission.

A last exit of animals now took place. From a many-angled array of outbuildings there erupted, with the shrieking that can sometimes be heard, a speckling of bats, dizzy in the warm afternoon. They went milling across the farmyard and over the fields and disappeared against the white cliff beyond. In the house the whistling stopped, and voice spoke to voice.

David went to the back door, which is usually the one that will open on a farm, and rapped on it. A large dusty moth crawled out of a crack in the stone-work above the door and flew off towards the sun.

'That's not a candle, stupid,' said David. Then the door opened, and he was blinking down at someone he could not see distinctly because his eyes had followed the dusty moth too far towards its flaming goal.

'I'm looking for Mr Babbacombe,' said David. 'This is Swallow Farm, isn't it? I'm from the Clandestine Insurance Company.'

'That'll be about the cows, then,' said the person who had opened the door. It was a female of some age or other and of some aspect or other: David could still not see anything distinctly.

'That's right,' he said. He liked her voice.

'Martin,' she said, 'where's Dad to?'

'On the land,' said another voice.

'You'd best come in then,' said this daughter of the claimant. Unless of course she had said 'Dad' as some mothers do when asking the children where their husbands are. She stepped back to let him in, and put herself in the way of the sunshine that came through a window.

He saw that she wore an old brown apron with a bib and a honey-coloured shirt with torn sleeves. He saw that she had flour on one cheek and a smut-mark from the oven on her chin, that her hair was a light caramel colour, that her eyes were blue or brown or grey or some natural colour, that she was making tea, that she was pouring him a cup, that she was giving him one, that she was speaking. But while he was in one way attending to her in the fullest possible manner, in another he was ignoring her. He was so intent on watching her that he forgot to listen.

'Well, you may stand if you wish,' she said. 'But there's the chair if you come to fancy it, there.'

'Oh yes,' said David. 'I was just thinking,' he added. 'About the cows; you know, the claim.'

'They're insured,' she said. 'Or did he forget to pay the premium?'

'Oh no, that's all right,' said David. He could see clearly now, and this must be Black Babbacombe's daughter. There was not much black about her, he thought, except for the impermanent smudge on her chin. She was still holding a cup of tea out to him. He reached out his hand, took the saucer she had touched, and dropped it straight on the floor.

'Well, there,' she said, putting out her hand vaguely as if to catch the ghost of the cup before it fell. David put his hand out vaguely too, and caught the hand. It was warm and floury.

'Will they pay out on that cup too?' she said, taking her hand away and bringing a cloth.

'Of course,' said David. 'Naturally. Anything like that.' But he was not thinking, he was not hearing the question. He did not mind what she said. He was in

38

love. He did not think it had happened before. There had been prophecies about it, that was all; hints in history, but not actuality for anyone until now.

5

Mr Babbacombe had not come in. Martin went on with homework in a sultry front room, while the insurance man sat in the kitchen and dropped a cup on the floor. He had gone after a long fruitless visit, Martin thought. He had left a claim form on the table and Jane had spilt milk on it. Bought milk, bought in Marret. Then, when a thundery rain had begun to spit down he had gone running among the drops, saying quite happily that he would return the next day. Martin and Jane both concluded that the steepness of the road had frightened him and made him leave his car at the top of the cliff. Mr Babbacombe did not come in even when the rain began to fall heavily. Martin looked through the window facing the town and could not see as far as the harbour. There were small boats idle and wet on the sea. They now and then threw dark shadows of themselves on the matt surface, when lightning reflected from a cloud.

'Gone up the pub,' said Jane. 'That's where he's to.'

'You're getting to talk common,' said Martin. 'Like him.'

'Well, what's the point of anything else?' said Jane.

40

Then she giggled, which was not her sort of noise.

'That's vulgar,' said Martin.

'It's all right if you do it properly,' said Jane. 'I've never done it for years, there don't ever come people to visit here friendly-like.'

'It's the curse on the place,' said Martin. 'Did you know there was a curse on the place?'

'I don't heed stories,' said Jane. 'Stories come in here and there isn't any way out for them, the road don't go no farther, that's all, so they hang about.'

'You know them, if you don't heed them,' said Martin. 'What are they?'

'Those Swallows,' said Jane. 'You know that one; you and him, you made it up, go on, didn't you?'

'No, never fear,' said Martin. 'I saw that, I did do.'

'Well, there's witches,' said Jane, taking a step towards him and opening her eyes wider. 'And there's hobgoblins and there's pixilated folk been here, and there's ordinary hauntings of ghosts, back and forth they go, back and forth, and there's the ghost horse, haven't you heard of that? It comes putting its head through the windows, upstairs and down, and if you see it you're to die. And there's things come out of the sea at night, when it have thundered and the moon gets out again, long they are, and narrow, and they creep.'

'Shut up,' said Martin, fascinated but terrified. Jane could always have him trembling and curled on the floor with a coat over his ears shouting to keep the noise of her voice out of his bones. 'What's true and what isn't?'

'Made that up,' said Jane. 'Just stories, mind, about the Swallows, and Mother said that Gran said ...'

'The one that didn't get burned up?' said Martin.

'That one,' said Jane. 'The old fools. But Gran said

that her mother said that if the animals left it was time for the folk to go. But I don't reckon the cows meant to go, so we shan't heed that either now.'

'Did you see them, then?' said Martin, sure that this was more teasing.

'I wasn't born, was I?' said Jane. 'That would be a hundred years ago, I dare say.'

Martin said nothing about the animals he and Stinking Tom had seen leave. The sight had been disturbing at the time, and had been a portent of some kind, and the adding to it of what Jane now said made it dangerous as well as disturbing. But to say it to Jane now would not make her believe it. She would know it was a feeble attempt to make her skin crawl in its turn, and Martin had never succeeded in altering her composure in that way.

The storm flickered its way inland. The rain lifted, and there was a new strong silence about the house. There seemed to be not even an insect to cut the air.

'I don't see the dogs or the cats,' said Jane. 'And those chicken have roosted in the cliff once more. Do you think they've all left like Gran's mother said?'

'Yes,' said Martin. 'I saw them go.' But it was not to be heard by Jane that night.

The sweetness of the storm stayed after it and lifted the dew of the sea on to the land and the smell of it in at the windows. The sun went down in a big transfused haze, a wide setting over land and sea. Martin went to bed and heard the tide wash against the cliffs a mile away, and the town clocks talk about ten o'clock and eleven o'clock, and saw the lights come up and go down again and stand along the harbour echoed in the sea.

He went to sleep. Some time later he woke up uneasy in complete darkness. There was an insistent ticking noise in the wall beside his bed. It was as if rows of miniature smiths were clouting in turn at some firm chisel or wedge or anvil, each blow driving the sound out farther. He listened, and soon it seemed as if the room were filled with the noise.

Then his window closed. He thought a stray breeze might have done it, until he recollected that the upper sash had been lowered, and could only be closed by lifting. No amount of rattling breeze would lift the window vertically, though it might have allowed it to fall if it had been the lower sash.

Then something ran through the room, opened the door, and slammed it shut, and then went on running for some distance longer than the house, shouted, and dwindled to nothing. Martin trembled, and heard the bed tremble with him. He sat up and the night air ran cold fingers across his sweated body. He reached across and put on the light from the switch by the door.

The window was open, as it had been. The door was open, as he had left it. Then the night ouside seemed to be looking in at him through the squares of the window, and to be waiting for him outside the open door, and he was afraid. He was mostly afraid of the thing that had run through the house. The ticking in the wall had stopped now.

He got right out of bed. By doing that he knew he was wide awake and not dreaming. He felt his weight on his feet and the cold of the nails in the floorboards. He stood by his bed and listened.

There was a single loud bang somewhere downstairs. That woke Jane. He heard her lamp being switched on, and saw the trail of its light through the crack at the hinge of her door. Her door opened, and it was Jane that came out of the room and not any other thing.

'Dad,' said Jane. 'What are you doing?' But it was not Mr Babbacombe downstairs. He was asleep in his bed, and not even drunk. Jane spoke to him from the landing, and he told her to get back to bed and stop her folly, he hadn't heard naught.

'I did,' said Martin, in a whisper.

'We'd best look,' said Jane. 'Come on, Martin, if he won't.'

Martin was not unwilling to go. With Jane there and awake it seemed to him that there could not be much wrong. He started to walk towards her. But one foot would not move.

'I'm caught, or something like,' he said. 'The floor's got hold of my foot.'

'Now, it's your folly,' said Jane.

'No, 'tis true,' said Martin. 'It's worse than hold, it's pulling at me, eating me, Jane.'

His right foot was free, but the left one was nipped by two of the floorboards where there was a join across. A T-shaped gap had hold of the sole of his foot behind the toes and was pulling mercilessly.

'Folly, I said,' said Jane. 'Stand on the other foot and don't play your cowardice on me, Martin.'

'Come and lift it yourself,' said Martin, sitting down and trying to pull the foot with his own hands. Jane saw that he was not manufacturing a condition, and came to pull with him.

' 'Tis true,' she said. 'Does it hurt then?'

'Cruel,' said Martin. 'Pinched, it is.'

Then the foot came loose, because, apparently, the boards shifted a little way apart. But a worse thing set in. A gap in the floor that ran under his left flank tightened up in turn, and gripped him intractably across the bottom.

'My arse,' he said.

'Now hush, be proper,' said Jane.

'That's what's pinched now,' said Martin.

44

'Get out,' said Jane, and she pulled at him as he sat there, and he came up. But a strip of pyjama trouser tore out, and so did a length of skin. Jane applied sticking plaster to the bottom and safety pins to the pyjamas. Before she had finished the pinning there was another report from downstairs. Martin put on his shoes and they went downstairs to look.

There was nothing disarrayed downstairs. In the unfamiliar bright but slightly browned light of the early hours of the morning they saw nothing out of place. Some soot had come down the chimney, but Jane reckoned the rain had brought that down.

'We'll have some tea,' said Jane. 'It'll be light in an hour.'

She switched on the electric kettle. Nothing happened while it sat heating, and she made the tea without any more noise. But as they began to sip it, sitting in the kitchen against the retained heat of the range, noises began again.

This time the dozen smiths were life-size, it seemed, and they were in the same wall again. They were trying to batter their way into the house from outside, or from what lay beyond that wall, an outhouse that used to be a stable.

Jane screamed. Martin thought that was the best thing to do, because neither of them dared move. Jane's cup had gone the way of another cup earlier on. Martin's stood on its saucer and shook at the frenzy of blows. Mr Babbacombe came downstairs in his shirt and trousers, asking what the hell was going on.

It was impossible to tell him; the noise had increased so much. Mr Babbacombe was about to go outside and deal with all twelve smiths when the noise stopped, and the shaking stopped. Once more something ran through the house, only through a longer house than the one here now, and laughed like an idiot as it went, and finished its course by tumbling, it seemed down a well that had no bottom and no water.

Then all was quiet again.

'Who the hell was that bugger?' said Mr Babbacombe.

6

'Rheumatism?' said Sergeant Lowes, wondering why a kipper at breakfast went on tasting like cigars for the rest of the morning. Could there have been confusion at the factory? 'If you said pneumonia I might have sympathy, but rheumatism is nothing to a lad your age.'

'My joints were chilled,' said Constable Zeal. 'Today I feel a lack of suppleness in them, as well as a twinge or two of pain.'

'I weep for you,' said Sergeant Lowes. 'Now you know the crime wave has really begun. But tell me more. Black Babbacombe threw you in the pond, did he?'

'A man of formidable strength and redoubtable temper,' said Constable Zeal.

'You won't doubt it any more, if that's what the word means,' said Sergeant Lowes. 'Go on, why haven't you got him locked up on several charges, like obstructing a police officer in the execution of his duty?'

'We'll have to prove a crime first,' said Constable Zeal. 'If you remember, you thought there might be a fraud in the offing, and I was looking into that. If there

47

isn't a fraud then I wasn't engaged in much of a duty.'

'We haven't even got reasonable grounds for thinking there was a fraud,' said Sergeant Lowes. 'It's just that I think of Black Babbacombe as a villain. It's been a funny family, lad. You know about his own mother's cremation, do you?'

'I have heard,' said Constable Zeal. 'It'd be illegal, that, of course.'

'No, I don't think so,' said Sergeant Lowes. Was there, he wondered, a whisker growing inwards from his right cheek, touching his tongue? Could such things be? 'They've always been atheists, or freethinkers, or one of those creeds, or worse.'

'Worse?' said Constable Zeal.

'Hypocrite, you are,' said Sergeant Lowes. 'You think there's nothing worse than not going to church. Has your beard started growing inwards yet?'

'Not yet, Sergeant,' said Constable Zeal. 'There's a limit to my hypocrisy.'

'The beard's a separate question,' said Sergeant Lowes. 'I'm talking about Black Babbacome and worse than atheism. You see, an atheist won't mind being buried in a churchyard because when he's dead he isn't around any more. But there are people who won't be buried there because of other things, other beliefs.'

'Like believing they're still alive,' said Constable Zeal. 'I don't want to be buried yet; I'm not dead.'

'But if you were,' said Sergeant Lowes. It came to him all at once that the ingrown beard touching his tongue was a small bone from the kipper wedged between teeth. He sucked at it. There was a taste like very old cigars. 'We could do with a cup of tea.'

'I could do with a cup of tea whether I am or not,' said Constable Zeal.

'Are what or not?' said Sergeant Lowes.

48

'Dead,' said Constable Zeal. 'You suggested that if I were dead we could do with a cup of tea.'

'If I were dead,' said Sergeant Lowes, 'it would be a question of spirits, ha ha. But I was telling you about Black B. They've got a cemetery out there, you know, right up on the cliff edge. They used to have their own chapel, but that went into the sea before my time. But the burial ground's still there, just part of one of the fields now. And I'm thinking that atheists don't need a chapel for anything, so what were they doing there?'

'Smuggling,' said Constable Zeal.

'No, not that. Or maybe,' said Sergeant Lowes. 'No, it was worshipping the Devil, or Witchcraft, or other evil practices.'

'But I suppose we aren't concerned very much with that now,' said Constable Zeal.

'No,' said Sergeant Lowes. 'It's just all in the back of my mind when I think of Black Babbacombe, and I know they're all a bad lot, the Babbacombe men. But it wouldn't be enough suspicion for anything, and I shouldn't have sent you off on that errand, I dare say, because he hasn't any reputation for fraud, only for being a Babbacombe. But if you can't get him for obstructing your investigation you can get him for common assault.'

'I doubt that,' said Constable Zeal. 'There were two witnesses.'

'Then it's made for you,' said Sergeant Lowes. He was longing for this conversation to end so that he could put several fingers in his mouth and pull out the fishbone. Was it right, he wondered, that you could wish on a fishbone that got stuck in your mouth?

'One witness is Babbacombe's son,' said Constable Zeal. 'The other is Thomas Millington-Boothe-Clough. I questioned him shortly after the incident and he

49

asserted that I was along at the time of the incident and had skidded from the road into one of the ponds.'

'Thomas Millington-Boothe-Clough,' said Sergeant Lowes. 'I tell you, Constable, there is such a thing as a criminal class, even if they never do anything criminal. There's Babbacombe and his family, and there's the Millington-Boothe-Clough lot, descended from the Duke of Omnium. If ever three surnames were sold for five farthings they are here. They'll say anything on oath, and anything off oath. It's no good trying anything in court with that set of facts. You'd better get Black B to throw you in again, and have some reliable witnesses ready first.'

'In China in the old days it was considered quite proper to hire witnesses to say the right thing, if necessary,' said Constable Zeal. 'This would seem to be a case where it might be a good principle to adopt.'

'Sure,' said Sergeant Lowes. 'The only thing against it is that we've never been given enough money for that sort of thing. We'll just have to try again. Anyway, I'm sure we'll get him on a charge of fraud before long. You wait, but don't wait in here, go and get the tea made.'

Constable Zeal went out. Sergeant Lowes put his fingers in his mouth and fished about for the bone. His fingers tasted of linoleum.

* * *

'Hush, Mr Hayman, do,' said Miss Slingsby. 'Mr Dawson is still reading his letters and you're much too cheerful.'

'Not cheerful at all,' said David. 'This is the disguise of a broken heart, I think.'

'Ah well,' said Miss Slingsby, through the rattle of yet another inventory being fed through her eyes and fingers and typewriter to permanent lodging on paper. 'That happens to us all at times. In this very room, Mr Hayman, was my heart broken.'

'Tell me,' said David. He was beginning to put papers away in his own desk. 'Who's been filling the place with creatures?' he asked, because when he opened a drawer a fly flew out and cracked its head on the window and lay aching on the floor below.

'When I was a little girl,' said Miss Slingsby, 'there was ever such a nice doctor living here with his family. This room was a nursery, and very pretty, with transfers on the walls and a toy cupboard. I only came here once, I think, but it was love at first sight. He was called Rodney, and he was a visitor too. It was a party, you know. I did think he was beautiful, and I told him so, I can remember my heart beating and my hair ribbon coming out with emotion. But he told me to go away, he didn't want girls playing with him, he was going to play with a model aeroplane. I've hated aeroplanes ever since.'

'So what did you do?' asked David. 'Where were you standing, where was he? Was your heart insured against breakages?'

'I think it has been ever since,' said Miss Slingsby. 'You men don't know what damage you do. The toy cupboard was in that recess there. It was ever so high, higher than the whole room is now, I'm sure. You know how things get smaller as you get older. Well, he was kneeling in front of it and I sat by the fire for a long time watching. Ah well, Sydney, it was a long time ago.'

'You said Rodney before,' said David.

'I know,' said Miss Slingsby. 'I can't remember quite what his name was. It might have been Brinley or Andy. A little thing like a name doesn't stop a girl from loving a man.'

No, it didn't, David thought. Miss Babbacombe was the nearest he could get to the name of the girl at the farm. In fact he had come to the office today in order to look in the Babbacombe file to see whether she was named. Miss Babbacombe was as handsome a name as any, of course, but there was something imprecise about it. There might, after all, be three more Miss Babbacombes, all great aunts of repellent strain.

There was nothing in the file to indicate what family Mr Babbacombe had. But of course it did not matter: he would be going to the farm again to collect the claim form. And in a little while he would be able to take the cheque to Mr Babbacombe.

'Mr Hayman,' Miss Slingsby was saying, 'will you please not do that to the files. How can you expect me to sort them out when I don't know where you've put any of them.'

'Oh dear me, I'm sorry,' he said.

'It's my belief you've fallen in love, Mr Hayman, said Miss Slingsby.

'It's my belief that she'd rather play with her pastry cutters and oven cloths,' said David. 'I hope I don't grow up to hate pastry cutters.'

'You could always use an ordinary knife,' said Miss Slingsby, rattling out a practical line or two of a letter and pulling the page from the typewriter. 'No, Mr Dawson will be glad to know about one or two of your visits yesterday, since you didn't ring back to the office except when you asked me about that client with the cows. I should have asked you then. Come on, Mr Hayman, let's get everything ready for Mr Dawson.'

* * *

'Babbacombe,' said a loud voice, and Martin opened his eyes to the bright walls of school. 'Don't go to sleep on the job, then,' said the Chemistry master. 'Or have you been manufacturing chloroform again?'

Martin woke up as well as he could. He had stayed awake but brittle until dinner time, but after that he had drooped and wanted to coil himself into some corner and sleep. After the noises in the night sleep would not come to him again. If he had dozed off some giant noise of his own breathing would call him terrified from sleep and set his heart thudding. In the end he had propped himself up against the now silent wall in the grey light of a cloudy dawn and waited until daylight. When his father had gone downstairs, and Jane followed him, he had felt safe enough to drift into a few moments' sleep, but not more than five minutes had been allowed him before Jane called to him to come down.

As well as being tired he was apprehensive of loud noises, and kept wondering what was behind walls and whether the wall would burst open and reveal something unimaginable.

Stinking Tom had been quiet about the thing Martin expected him to be loudest about and most scornful, the exodus of animals from the farm lands. Perhaps, Martin thought, he had tried the story out on someone and been told it was too fanciful. At any rate no word of it seemed to be around in school.

'Anything else happened?' Stinking Tom had asked at one moment when they were alone in the school yard.

'Haunted,' said Martin, without considering whether Tom was a friend or a bullying acquaintance. He was both, of course, but mostly acquaintance. He only bullied because he came from a very rough family who had not thought of other ways of expressing their opinion.

'Ghosts and that?' he said.

'All night,' said Martin.

'Are they coming again tonight?' asked Tom.

'I can't tell,' said Martin. 'How could I know?'

'Just asked, then,' said Tom.

*   *   *

David came down to Marret in the afternoon, making all his ordinary calls on the way. He telephoned the office from beside the harbour. From here he could see the headland and Swallow Farm. He watched them as he listened to the ringing of the bell at the far end.

'Clandestine,' said Miss Slingsby in one ear, and a seagull yodelled resoundingly in the other. 'Yes, Mr Hayman, Mr Dawson would like to speak to you.'

'Perhaps your friend's name was Henry,' said David.

'What?' said Miss Slingsby.

'Not Sydney or Rodney or Brinley but Henry.'

'I'm sure I couldn't say,' said Miss Slingsby. David thought that Miss Slingsby was probably cured of her broken heart by now, or of that particular one.

'Dawson,' said Mr Dawson. 'We've a call from Arbor Farm, Marret, about insurance of stock. They have

54

thirty cows, and there's been some sort of accident and they've got in touch with us. Ten of them have been electrocuted, I gather.'

'More cows,' said David. 'That's a co-incidence.'

'Is it?' said Mr Dawson. 'You look carefully into this, Mr Hayman, you look very carefully into it. We may be faced with Fraud on a large scale, and when we are faced with Fraud we do not have to pay. The farmer's name is Hagblow.'

'Hagblow,' said David. 'Yes, I know the name.' He put the telephone down thoughtfully. Mr Dawson's voice stopped falling out of it. Now what, he thought, if all the Babbacombe family and the Hagblow family are in this together? What can I do about loving Miss Babbacombe?

7

What does Miss Babbacombe look like? he wondered
as he drove out through the town. Here I am, Miss
Babbacombe, if that's you : boy, bring that smudge of
black and see whether it fits her chin. There, fits it like
a glove, if you see what I mean, Miss Babbacombe.
Here I am, madam, David Lloyd Hayman, aged twenty-
six, your friendly insurance man, and I'd like to give
you life cover. Do you, David, take this woman, do you,
Barbara—it could be Barbara, or it could be anything.
What other names are there? But he could think of no
others, except Rodney and Sydney.

He missed the turning and had to go back again.
There had been no man hedging to remind him and
slow him down. What if there were no road now? he
wondered. Was it all, could it have been, some strange
dream?

Then he had to open the field gates one by one.
Today there rose no dripping policeman to advise him,
there approached no rout of refugee hedge-dwellers.
All seemed a calm peace, a devout and holy silence
seemed to rest on the land below the cliff. One could
live here, he said to himself, pausing at the top of the

slope. Two could live here, in fact. He saw the farm below, and the door of it open and a curl of smoke sitting above the chimney. He drove down.

There was a bump at the bottom of the slope. It looked as if someone had recently dug a trench across and then filled it in with white chalk from the cliff, but not quite full, so that there was a step down and a step up. It had not been there the day before. No doubt it had something to do with the water supply, perhaps the domestic water was tasting strange after the cows had drowned in the pond.

He came to the house and turned the car about. Silence greeted him, and no dog barked. A moment of discomfort came to him then, but he put it aside. Now, once more, he was to meet her. Did she look the same still, and how was it that she looked in any case? He walked to the door, tapped on it, and stepped inside.

'Oh,' said Jane. 'You're back then. You'll be wanting that paper, and I wonder what Dad has done with it. He's in, but he has somebody, a friend, like, in there with him.'

'Will they be long, do you think?' said David. What a banal question in response to the utterance of a goddess, he thought. Clean face this time, she had, and what baking there was seemed to have been abandoned for the time being; the bowls of beaten egg and the moon-cratered flour were laid aside, the salt packet had tipped over and the contents alped out over the table.

' 'Tes only Jemmy,' said Jane. 'He'll be off directly and help his brother up their place.'

'Stop talking so rough, Jane,' said another person who was in the room. It was Martin, sitting by the window in a high-backed chair, reading his homework. With Mr Babbacombe and Jemmy in the other room he had been driven to the kitchen to work. 'She's putting it on a bit,' said Martin, looking round the side of the chair. 'She does. It's because of Jemmy, I think.'

'Don't 'ee listen, Sir, Master, Lord,' said Jane, throwing half an eggshell at each honorific and Martin as she spoke.

'You were busy in the kitchen yesterday too,' said David, taking no notice of extravagant behaviour. 'Do you do much of the housekeeping?'

'I do it all,' said Jane. 'Mother's been gone since I was his age, and I began then.'

'Gone?' said David. 'What do you mean?'

'Died,' said Jane. 'And buried in the churchyard.'

'Yes, of course,' said David, not really meaning anything but using the words as something quiet to say.

'We mostly get buried up in the fields,' said Jane. 'That's the way we manage hereabouts, Babbacombes.'

'I was wondering what your name was, yesterday,' said David. 'It isn't in our records at the office.'

'Jane Babbacombe, so far,' said Martin. 'Isn't it?'

'That's how *I* choose,' said Jane. 'Well, no, you wouldn't have my name there. I never was insured, I hope. I wouldn't fancy anything like that.'

'Come now,' said David, 'I can't hear anything against the insurance principle, can I?'

'Too many cows get struck by lightning,' said Jane. 'I couldn't say ours do, because what happened to them must have been real, they couldn't have made it up, Dad and Martin. However, you can talk to Dad when he comes out. Martin, go out and bring some more small wood directly, and some coal.' Martin dropped his book and went out. 'It isn't cold,' said Jane, 'but the current's gone off and I'll have to cook on the range, but of course I never lit it today with the day

58

being so warm and having such a bad night, down here before dawn we were with a ghost.'

'Tell me about it,' said David. He wondered why people had to become real, divinity have drawbacks. Why Venus from the misty sea should speak with such a rustic tone and believe thrivingly in superstition: ghosts. When she mentioned the ghost her eyes woke up with a scared excitement.

'I don't like to recall it,' she said. 'We all heard it, and we never had one before, not in the house. It was beating down the wall tremendously, just there, and then it got up and ran all through the house and faded away, and that was all. But Martin heard more. It woke Dad, and we sat round and had tea when it had got away.'

The door to the room beyond opened, and two men came out. Martin came back into the kitchen as well, with his firewood. The big fat man would be Mr Babbacombe, thick trousers, thick shirt, string for a belt, bald head with white skin on top from wearing a hat at all times, and boots that struck sparks even in this daylight from the kitchen floor. The other man was that Hagblow David had seen the previous day cutting the hedge.

'You never got your can of tea, Jemmy,' said Mr Babbacombe.

'I can't boil a kettle on nothing,' said Jane. 'I suppose you misremembered to pay the electricity bill, Dad.'

'I think you paid it yourself,' said Mr Babbacombe. 'They'll fix it back as soon as they can, Jane. Well, Jemmy, we only have the electric kettle and we haven't the electric, and you know I don't keep a drop of anything else in the house, or not for very long if I do set out on a store of it.'

'I won't have it in, either,' said Jane.

'I told you,' said Mr Babbacombe. 'I told you, Jemmy.'

'I be off, then,' said Jemmy Hagblow. 'Afternoon to you, Sir. I reckon you got yourself here one way and another,' he said to David.

'Yes, indeed, Mr Hagblow,' said David, who knew all the names he had heard and the faces they belonged to. The name Hagblow was firmly in mind today even before it belonged to Jemmy. Jemmy went off slowly, being edged out by Mr Babbacombe.

David stood aside, and wondered. Hagblow, Babbacombe, nine lost cows, ten dead cows. Was there a connexion between them? Could there be a plot? Of course it was impossible to think that Jane had anything to do with it. But even if she had no guilty knowledge (if there was a plot) she would still be the daughter of a guilty man. At the moment the plot seemed simple, though not very clever. Farmer Babbacombe says he has lost his cows without trace, taken by fairies or the great sea monster. He is paid the insurance money. Farmer Hagblow says he has about the same number of dead cows (perhaps they kill them, but, question, how does a farmer electrocute his cows?) and he gets paid for them. But what really happened was that the Babbacombe cows were walked to the Haglow field and there shocked to death, and the week before that the Hagblow cows were taken to another market and sold. So between them the farmers get the sale money, from good cows, the insurance money from a lot of old cows dead in a field, and another lot of insurance money from the same cows who didn't vanish into a mysterious pool, by any manner of means.

Mr Babbacombe came back. 'That were Jemmy,' he said. 'We were making arrangements.'

'Never!' said Jane. 'Well, who'd 'a thought it?'

60

David feared that these were guilty-sounding remarks. But he was comforted by the thought that if the two men had been able to think out their scheme then they would also be able to keep themselves from saying incriminating things.

'I'm not a cow,' said Jane. And that was another remark that could mean conspiracy and guilt. Or it could mean something else quite different, and much worse. It could mean that Jemmy had been here trying to make some arrangement about Jane. But there was no time to think of everything now.

'Where's your bloody bit of paper?' said Mr Babbacombe. 'You'll be from the Insurance. Jemmy said he spoke to you yesterday. If you just happened to be enquiring about me round about, young man, let me tell you it ain't none of your business. I have a true legal arrangement with you and you've to pay over the money like it says, and the sooner the better, I say.'

'I asked Mr Hagblow the way yesterday,' said David.

'I do know that,' said Mr Babbacombe. 'It's like a warning, see. I handled one man rough yesterday, prying and interfering and making out this and that about the matter. I've had no hanky panky with you, so don't you have none with me.'

'No question of it,' said David. 'I've come to help you with the claim form. It's not many people who are happy at filling forms, and that's all I've come for at the moment, and to have a look at the place where it happened.'

'No statements, mind,' said Mr Babbacombe. 'It's statements that hang folks.'

'I hope not,' said David. 'But there's a space on the form for an account of the circumstances, and of course they have to have that at the Head Office in London.'

'Well, where is the paper, girl?' said Mr Babbacombe.

61

'And I'll go through it with you,' said David.

There was no form to be found. Jane said she had had it on the table that very day, Clandestine Insurance, Claim Form. It was no longer on the table.

'It was there when I began cooking,' said Jane.

It became obvious, after a time, that Martin had lit the fire with it. 'I picked it up off the floor if I did,' he said. 'It isn't like money, is it?'

'Of course it is, you varmint,' said Mr Babbacombe. 'Like never so much money as you saw, lad.'

'No, it's nothing,' said David. 'I'll get another from the car, just outside.'

He lied as he said that, and he knew it. But he went to the car and looked in his brief-case. There was a bundle of claim forms there, but ran his fingers over them and closed the case. He made a pretence of looking in the pockets of the car, and in his own pockets, but that was a lie too. He came back to the kitchen. 'Of all things,' he said. 'I don't seem to have any with me. I think I'd better come again tomorrow. Or you can come to the office, Mr Babbacombe, if you like.'

'I don't want any trips out,' said Mr Babbacombe. 'Jane could come, if she's a mind to.'

'That would be very nice,' said David. 'But I think you would fill the form better, Mr Babbacombe.' Then he said he was sorry again about not having the forms, and drove away. The trench at the bottom of the cliff seemed to jolt the car much more as he went across it this way. He thought it was because he went over it faster to get a run at the hill.

* * *

Sergeant Lowes looked at the town with its turned evening shadows. An oniony belch settled into the air round him. He plodded on with his typing, using his right hand. The left hand went to his mouth and fingered that persisting whisker of a kipper bone, still there but flavourless. The morning brought the percentages up, he thought. Thereafter all that came along was recurrences and repeats of things already known, as if the crimes accumulated at night lay fermenting into eructations (he had this good word for a belch from a Stomach Tablet Bottle) that came to the notice of the tasting mind through the day as the law digested the crime and the criminals. No doubt too rich a diet of events and lawlessness would overload the machine and lay it low with a bilious attack of some kind.

Constable Zeal came in. Sergeant Lowes told him some of his thoughts.

'Here's one for a nightcap,' said Constable Zeal. 'There's been ten more cows lost.'

'They should provide them with maps,' said Sergeant Lowes.

'Yes indeed,' said Constable Zeal. 'These cows belong to a Mr Hagblow of Arbor Farm.'

'Indeed,' said Sergeant Lowes in his turn. 'And Arbor Farm is next to Swallow Farm, and one and one make two.'

'Two point five, perhaps,' said Constable Zeal.

'That's lovely to sleep on,' said Sergeant Lowes. 'Most delicate and rare. You can go and get a statement from Mr Hagblow. And take a swimming lesson before you go, Constable.'

8

The man waited at the gate. David saw that it was Jemmy Hagblow, not opening the gate yet, a thing that David thought any courteous person would do. But he had to stop the car. Jemmy came to the window.

'If you be going up to the road and down-along, it might be I could ride with you,' he said. 'Seemingly.'

'Certainly,' said David. It would be a good opportunity to speak about cows before seeing them. 'Will you open the gate?'

'I might do,' said Jemmy. 'But perhaps I didn't ask you for a ride and you didn't say yes or no.'

'That's true,' said David. 'You didn't ask and I didn't reply.'

'More like two people saying things,' said Jemmy. 'Not being too free with each other when still strangers, like.'

'That's it,' said David. 'But I'll give you a lift, and if you'll open the gate I'll drive through and wait for you the other side.'

'Now, that's an arrangement,' said Jemmy. 'I like arrangements.'

He opened the gate. David drove through and

waited. Jemmy closed the gate and came to sit beside him.

'You've got a brother, have you?' said David.

'Direct personal questions,' said Jemmy. 'Well, yes, I have, called Jacko; direct personal answer.'

'I'm looking for Arbor Farm,' said David. Jemmy was silent for a time.

'That's where I'm bound,' he said. 'Milking time. However, I don't see what to do but take you there, because that'll suit you and it'll suit me.' But he did not seem happy at the idea, David thought.

'If anything else would suit you better, tell me,' said David.

'Nothing would be better,' said Jemmy. 'It's just that things don't so often come out rational; what you want being what I want. I'm sure to have to make up for it somewheres else, lose here, gain there; more hedge, less hay.'

'That's true,' said David. 'It's all a matter of making things fit each other, good and bad mixed together. Tell me about your brother's farm.'

'Direct personal statements again,' said Jemmy. 'You won't sharpen yourself on a poor countryman, will you?'

'No,' said David. 'But I have to visit your brother about his cows.'

'You don't smell like a vet,' said Jemmy. 'Direct personal negative statement.'

'I'm not a vet,' said David. 'I'm from the insurance company, and there's been an accident with the cows.'

'Not that there continuous aversion?' said Jemmy.

'No,' said David. 'Electrocution, I heard, and ten cows dead.'

'Well I be damned,' said Jemmy. 'I don't know why you have to go to Black Babbacombe to hear that, and if they be dead I don't know why you have to insure them, they'm worthless then. And besides it won't be Jacko's fault, 'twill be the supply company letting the juices down out of the wires all deadly. But that Babbacombe, he done it, killed off his own, kill off ours, we shan't be safe our direct personal selves no more, sitting there the old toad saying naught to me that has to milk them and laying down his terms.'

'What were the terms about?' said David.

'Oh, that *is* a real direct personal matter,' said Jemmy. 'I can't say aught of that.' But there was such a sickly grin on him as he spoke that David knew it must have something to do with Jane. Or, a sense of logic told him, it could still be some finagling with the cows. They came to the road and Jemmy opened the gate and said they were to turn left, 'Downalong.'

Arbor Farm was a mile towards the town, down towards the sea again. David asked why it was called Arbor Farm, and learnt that it was near the harbour. They came to the house and got out of the car. Jemmy had an exchange of indirect impersonal remarks, such as: 'There might be cows down over in Parkman's Patch this time of day.' Answered by: 'You can tell the time there, seemingly.'

'That means turmuts,' said Jemmy. 'You can tell the time by turmuts, see.'

At length it was determined where the cows were. In fact, by looking about, David had seen clearly that several vans and a tractor and a number of people had gathered two fields away and were intent on something.

The group sorted itself out as David came near. There was a vet in his white coat, accompanied by a smaller-sized Jemmy, who must be Jacko. There was a trio of knacker's men taking the bodies of cows on to a wagon, and there were five men from the Electricity Board dealing with wires.

David could see that it was to be one of the unsatisfactory claims where the company would pay out nothing and the farmer would get nothing for several years, because the people to blame were the Electricity Board, whose wires had trailed on the ground, and the fighting in court would last a decade.

'You know where he heard that old tale, Jacko,' said Jemmy to his brother, 'he heard it down at Black Babbacombe's and come on here to see about it.'

'He en't welcome then,' said Jacko. 'Howsomever.'

'I'm sure I am,' said David. 'Clandestine Insurance, Mr Hagblow . . . My name's Hayman, and I think you rang the office about your trouble.'

'What's this about Babbacombe, then?' said Jacko. 'You get off with you, Jem, there's a score of cows to milk yet down along over.'

'It's nothing to do with Babbacombe,' said David. 'He has his own troubles, but I knew about yours before I went to see him, and he knows nothing about this.'

'He might remarkably know all sorts,' said Jacko. 'But I have the vet here, telling me what these cows adied of, and it wasn't no fancy plunging in the Swallows neither.'

'He's a direct sort of man, this Insurance,' said Jemmy, who had not gone yet. 'Tell him straight and personal, Jacko.'

'I will,' said Jacko. 'Mister Clandestine, Black Babbacombe be at the bottom of this, it's like his cunning ways. And don't you hearken to his tales about they Swallows. It stands to reason nothing ever happened like it, no, not by nature. He had a hand in it himself did Black Babbacombe. And now this. You know where this line goes, out there across the fields? Why, down to Black Babbacombe's place, no less, and it's his current that came down and killed so many of my herd. Babbacombe have sucked it down to himself and then released it back and spread out destruction on me and mine. Saying, likely, that if he lose, we lose, I burn my hedges, you burn your hay, that's his creed, and all that cauldron of them down there.' Then he shouted at Jemmy, who was still standing by: 'Get away to the shippon, Jem, and stop there, and don't you collude no more with Babbacombe; there's been plenty of that.'

David went to talk to the vet, who was examining another dead cow. They talked about the deaths, and the vet was sure that electricity had been the cause in all cases. It does not take much electricity to kill a cow. Then he talked to the Electricity Board men. Something was badly astray with the line, the foreman said. You would think, he suggested, that a great hand had been at the far end and pulled firmly and suddenly, so that the wire unravelled itself and strands came down to touch the earth, making the whole field lethal to anything not wearing boots. A man had gone along the rest of the line to see what else was wrong with it. It was the foreman's private opinion that some accident with a farm tractor had pulled a post away and brought the present circumstance about. Like as not, he said, the tractor belonged to this farm and had been on this farm's land. David said that would complicate the insurance, though not so much as if the Board had been to blame.

The exploring electrician returned from his survey of the line. He had been to the cliff top and then down to Swallow Farm. He said that the line was not broken except in this one place, but that the posts had all been pulled crooked, even if they looked straight from here. They had not been buried deeply enough in the beginning, he said. The foreman told him to say no more now, but get the wires joined up and they would test the line and put current through. The whole line would have to be shifted in any case, because Jack Hagblow would not have it on his land any more.

Constable Zeal came up and joined the party now, having his own look round. Jacko nodded to him, Constable Zeal nodded to David and came to ask him what he was doing here. David explained who he was. Constable Zeal said that he might be getting in touch with the office, if the office didn't get in touch with the police first. Then Constable Zeal nodded in the general direction of everybody and rode off again.

*　　*　　*

Swallow Farm sat and sweated darkness, shedding shadow out of its tissue. Round it hung the faint dark of twilight, and high above a cloud in a cleared tract of sky picked up a trace of set sun, fading as cloud and sun travelled further apart.

Then one of the dark pores closed within the house. Jane had found and lit a candle. It now was the lone flame beneath the cliffs, because the fire had been allowed to sink to a frail cinder in the hot evening.

Outside were no animals, but tracking along a hedge bottom were two ovals that bobbed and glanced four feet from the ground, with no features in this light, no bodies to support the ovals, and no sound. A closely-approached observer would know by one of his senses that here was Stinking Tom and probably Pewter.

They had come along the cliff path and down the road, and were now making their way round the house

69

to a convenient window. They stopped for a moment and giggled briefly, as if the hedgehogs had returned, and went on. On the night air, now drifting from land to sea, came some sort of thumping noise from the cliffs. They paused, but hearing no more, moved on again.

They saw Jane by candlelight reading a magazine; Martin opposite taking notes from a book; Mr Babbacombe breathing heavily in sleep in a chair; the tired fire like a dead cat in the grate.

'Any time,' said Stinking Tom. Pewter nodded. Now the white ovals that had been their faces grew whiter and larger : they were drawing over their heads white cloths, pillow cases. They were blind with them on but that did not matter, or they had not noticed : they certainly had not foreseen it.

'One, two, three,' said Tom. And both of them set up a long screeching, and bobbed about among the herbs of the garden in what they thought was a realistic manner.

What happened was startling, though not entirely the result of the screeching. At that moment the Electricity Supply Company reconnected the current, and almost all the lights in the farm went on. Light dazzled and noise startled those inside. Jane knocked the candle over and grabbed for it as it fell in case the light went with it. Martin leapt up and cracked his head on the mantelpiece. Mr Babbacombe woke up, diagnosed the noise outside as varmints come haunting, and went to the cupboard for his shotgun.

The varmints come haunting knew there was light, but did not know there was enough of it spilling from the windows (as if the sweating fever of the house's darkness had broken) to reveal them in their antic trousers and grimed pillow cases. They danced and shrieked on.

Mr Babbacombe came to the open window, wasted no time on shouting, and fired the first barrel up into the air.

There was a double result to that. The cluster of lead shot, not very far spread, punched a piece out of the overhead electricity cable. The lights went out. One loose end of cable sprang back, coiled round the gun, forced its barrel low, and led Mr Babbacombe's hand to fire it whether he meant to or not. The two ghosts, silent for a startled moment, began again their cries, with a different intonation. The other end of the wire, still live, curled down to the ground, touched a water pipe so that a spark jumped from the grate in the house, which heated the water, to the fender, which contacted the floor. The wire bounced off the pipe, and tangled with another obstruction, and knocked that down with a heavy thud and a sigh and a small ringing noise.

Silence came as if there had never been anything else. Then there was a whimper and another whimper from outside. Mr Babbacombe let fall the gun and tried to speak. He had difficulty because the recoil of the second shot had winded him. He was wondering if he had been blinded too. He collected his thoughts, and sought to see, and saw.

'You buggers out there,' he said, 'what are you doing? I can see you still.'

'Oh God, I be dead,' said Stinking Tom. 'I fancy.'

'No no, 'tis I that be dead,' said Pewter. 'What hast done, Babbacombe, murderer?'

Jane found the matches and lit the caught candle. Martin sat and rubbed his head. Jane took the candle to the window and held it up. Two figures outside were discarding squarish shirts, she thought, and stepping forward.

'Shot them,' said Mr Babbacombe. 'Somehows. Right

71

and left, I reckon.' They came to the window and were hauled in. All their limbs were working, and they could see and hear and talk. At first they seemed un-injured, but Pewter gradually revealed what he assumed was a bullet hole. Jane looked, and reckoned a piece of flinty gravel had torn his trousers and grazed his ankle. Tom thought that one whole arm had been torn off, but it was still attached to him and unmarked but for a bruise. His sleeve was a little burnt, and that was all.

'You can be off, then,' said Mr Babbacombe. 'I don't owe you no hospitality this time, but you might get some next. Come to stay, you might just, in that place out on the cliff top. We've a right to bury folk there, surely, and I wouldn't charge you two no fees; glad to do it for naught.'

The two boys began to leave, Pewter limping and Tom holding his stunned arm. They were not at the door when the house moved under their feet, and a noise like a cannon shot began under the floor, moving about from stone to stone, of the kitchen, and then out of the kitchen and into the other room. Then it was in the wall behind the dresser, so that the plates seemed to whirr on their edges as they were stood. The cups and jugs began to leave their hooks and fall one or two at a time on to the ground, where they broke in separate notes in a slow random arpeggio.

They watched, all expecting any moment that the back of the dresser would be burst through by some visitant, some horror.

But what approached came from behind them. The outer door of the kitchen opened and a dark figure moved slowly in.

9

Miss Slingsby was too calm, too attentive to her work, thought David. She was not inquiring about the things uppermost in his mind, but wanting to know about Endowment Policies and Whole Life Policies and all the routine calls of the previous day. The office was too still, too much a backwater, too far inland, too remote from the streams and currents of real life. He went on telling her about the everyday matters, keeping the more interesting ones to the end.

Before he got to them Mr Dawson finished reading his letters and came through looking for him. Instead of telling Miss Slingsby all about the Babbacombe family and the Hagblows, as people not as insured persons, he had to discuss them with Mr Dawson as mere claimants, as business.

'Pending a resolution of the matter,' David found himself saying, wondering again what 'pending' really meant, 'I propose the Company take no further action initiating payment of these claims. It is not beyond possibility that collusion at least, and possibly conspiracy, are taking place.'

'Yeah,' said Mr Dawson. 'We'll hang on a bit and see

how it goes. We can't be paying out all at once if they're fiddling us. You go down there again now and sort it all out. You don't have to prove anything before paying out. If you feel it's all right that's good enough. It's when the company refuses to pay out that they've to have a good case, fit for the court.'

'The electrocution is the difficult one,' said David. 'We can't tell whether it's the Board's fault or an accident or something the farmer's done, this Jacko Hagblow.'

'It's what you're paid for,' said Mr Dawson. 'Work at it until you know.'

'In any contingency, whatever considerations ...' David began, but the telephone rang. Mr Dawson picked it up and said to David, 'That's enough of your fancy words.'

'Dudley!' said the telephone reprovingly.

'Not you, dear,' said Mr Dawson, waving David to sit down again because he had not wanted to wait during a domestic conversation. The conversation was one-sided, though, and consisted of Mr Dawson saying: 'Yes. Yes. Yes. Yes. Yes. Yes. Yes. Goodbye. Dear. Goodness, well,' and then putting the telephone down again. David wondered whether it was possible that in fact he was talking to Miss Slingsby and that they had arranged to do it like this to distract suspicion away from an affair.

'It's nearly time to tell the police,' said Mr Dawson, and David wondered for a moment still along the lines he was on already, and thought the police might have to be told about Miss Slingsby and Mr Dawson. For illegal telephone conversations, perhaps.

'There was a policeman at one scene the day before yesterday,' said David. 'Babbacombe had thrown him into the fatal pond. And the same one, I think, was

74

there yesterday at the other farm. But I think it was curiosity in both cases, because they are both strange stories, and they're strange folk down there. There's . talk of witchcraft, you know.'

'There's a standard clause in the Equatorial African Company's Policies for payment for not being able to attend to means of livelihood while changed into the form of another animal by means of witchcraft,' said Mr Dawson. 'It was found difficult to make sure of the facts of each case, that was the trouble. I heard that the Frog and Toad Insurance Company issue cover to their members in case they are turned into Princes by being kissed by Princesses. I think it happens quite often in woodland places.'

'I'll make a note of it,' said David, getting up and going: Mr Dawson was puzzling him again.

Miss Slingsby was working, one eye on the page, one on him.

'What about Dudley?' said David, when he had closed Mr Dawson's door.

'What about it?' said Miss Dawson.

'Name of the boy you fell in love with,' said David. 'Rodney, or Sydney.'

'*He's* called Dudley,' said Miss Slingsby. 'No, it wasn't Dudley, or if it was I'm glad he played with his aeroplane, and even if it wasn't I still would be, fancy sitting at home where he lives and some other woman being in this room with his history of playing not with aeroplanes.'

*　　*　　*

Marjoram, thought Sergeant Lowes. That was it,

75

marjoram. A toothful of marjoram, and that would be from the breakfast sausages. A convulsion among the breakfast sausages sent a belch up into his mouth, and echoed the marjoram that was in the tooth. Now, if sausage skins were made from the insides of animals, and we ate the sausages, how come we could digest their insides, when, really, most animals could eat far more indigestible things than we could? Why didn't the sausage skins take us over and digest us, instead of us digesting them? Sergeant Lowes thumped himself in the region of the third button down and belched gently once more. He looked out over the town and wondered when the revolution would begin, when the food would start to take over, when soup would be master, when chips would be anointed with holier fluids than vinegar, when there would be a large cauliflower in charge of this police station instead of Superintendent . . .

Constable Zeal came in. He limped. He was bandaged and had sticking plaster on his face. He was pale.

'What's the matter, man?' said Sergeant Lowes. 'Have you been set on by rioting jellies, or bitten by a wounded spaghetti?'

'It's not a laughing matter,' said Constable Zeal. 'Not for me, not today. I would have reported last night, but I went to the doctor instead.'

'Where did this happen?' said Sergeant Lowes, looking out with angered eyes towards the land beyond the town. 'Swallow Farm?'

'Yes,' said Constable Zeal.

'Right,' said Sergeant Lowes. 'We'll have him in, Black B, and we'll keep him here until we've got something that'll stick. You wait here, I'll get a car sent down, and we'll sort that mischief out.'

'No, no,' said Constable Zeal, quietly, because he

had a suspected cracked rib tied tight. 'They haven't done any of this, it just happened there, that's all. It wasn't a person did this, it was the ground, it was an accident.'

'Report to me now,' said Sergeant Lowes. 'You can go home and write it all down afterwards. Go on, start when you left here yesterday, to see Jack Hagblow and his little lot of insurance fiddle.'

Constable Zeal recounted how he had gone on a pedal cycle, since the moped was still out of action and not yet repaired. He had gone to Arbor Farm and looked about. The scene had been distressing, with ten dead cows in one place, and Mr Hagblow had seemed genuinely upset, and Constable Zeal had not tried to take any statement from him then, recalling from past experience what might happen if he spoke too soon to a worried and angered farmer. He had gathered that some sort of blame was attached to Black Babbacombe, and that Hagblow was inclined to blame him in some illogical manner. In consequence he had then ridden off towards Swallow Farm, getting there in the late dusk. In fact, being so near, he had gone home first and had a bite of supper.

Swallow Farm had appeared quiet from the top of the cliff. It had been a pleasant ride through the darkening air, though a little warm. Since he was on a farm track he did not put on the lamps, and coasted along in the grey light. He stopped at the top of the cliff and listened. Some way back inland he could hear the voices of the electricity engineers reconnecting the wires. Down by Swallow Farm there was nothing, unless a couple of dogs with white faces were crossing the yard. In the farm a small light showed up, flickering then steadying. A candle had been lit.

Constable Zeal rode down the hill in the dark, swooping through it and feeling the warm air cool itself against his eyes. He leaned over on the curves, and as the ground levelled out he began to pedal hard, to negotiate the little rise between the Swallows.

He went into the trench that David had bumped over already that evening. The car had recovered at once. But Constable Zeal's bicycle had been under power, had been turning a corner, had been leaning to one side. He fell off it, somersaulted, and landed on his back at the edge of the biggest Swallow, getting one shoulder wet. The bicycle bounded about as if it were dangling from a rope, anteloping in the road and then heading for the second Swallow, where it lay in much the same attitude and position as Constable Zeal in the first Swallow. It had wet handlebars.

Constable Zeal got up, counted himself, recovered the bicycle, and walked the rest of the way to the farm. He looked at the depression in the road as he went, and decided that no one could be blamed for it, only for falling into it. Nobody would confess to riding down a farmtrack without lights, unless nothing untoward occurred.

He had come into the yard and was standing there leaning on the bicycle, feeling shaken and groggy still, when a vile noise started the other side of the farm. It had alarmed him for a second, and then he had thought it must be cats or boys, nothing more than that. He did not know whether it was anything to do with him, or whether he could do anything about it even if it were. He thought he would go on standing and letting his head swim in the darkness.

Then the farm lights suddenly lit themselves, both in the house and out in the shippon. Constable Zeal closed his eyes against the outdoor lamp on the eaves: it was too bright for him just now. Just as he closed them there was the report of a gun and the house and shippon lights went out.

There was a sudden double throb underfoot, and another gunshot, and a hard cord swished through the air and flung itself round him and the bicycle and began to bite and hurt and flash sparks at him. He stepped away from it, breaking through the bicycle as if it were a bush, and crawled to one side. The thing did not follow him, but stayed with the bicycle, striking loud sparks from it. He saw that a wire hung down from the air, its end on the back wheel that still spun gently. Each time a spoke went under the wire there was a spark.

Constable Zeal stood up once more. He began to walk with care towards the farm, not wanting to come on any more wire. As he began to walk there came the sound of some disturbance from within. He took a breath, ready to speak, and thought he had been stabbed in the chest. Then he reckoned he had cracked a rib, and went on.

The noise continued. There was the breaking of crockery in it. It was his duty to intervene at once. Without knocking on the door he walked into the farm kitchen.

Five faces turned towards him. He saw how everyone had been standing peaceably, and that no physical act of violence was going on. All the same, the noise continued, and appeared to come from the dresser against the wall. From the dresser the cups were falling. Steadily the candle flame stood on the table and shone on all.

There was a diminishing of the noise, a silence, a shaking of the floor, and then the sound of goblins or trolls going through the house, one after the other, running the length of it, close by Constable Zeal, but not appearing. They ran the length and more, and came again and again. Constable Zeal turned himself slowly and walked out of the house, and listened outside. Here too the ghostly olympic went on, growing fainter and fainter but not further away, and ending as if all the runners had jumped down a shaft together.

Then he had gone in and spoken to the Babbacombe family, who were all alarmed by the events. Mr Babbacombe had picked up his gun from outside the window and put it away. On being questioned by Constable Zeal he said he had discharged it to discourage night-owls. Two boys present, namely Millington-Boothe-Clough and Pewter, had then left and had refused to make any comment or to explain their presence. Constable Zeal had then left himself, and Miss Jane Babbacombe had run after him with the candle, which enabled him to remove the input cable from his bicycle, where it had fallen after, presumably, being broken by a gunshot.

Sergeant Lowes said that was a matter for the Electricity Board. Constable Zeal said he did not doubt it, and went on to say that the haunting did not trouble them much, but she feared that some of the townspeople might come and cause trouble. It had happened before when she was a child and she had always dreaded its recurrence.

'Time of the cremation,' said Sergeant Lowes. 'There was a bit of hoo-ha about it. Dafties against Barmies, I think. Well, the presence of a uniform usually stops that sort of thing. You aren't any good for anything else. When you've written your report take that old van with radio and go down there and keep an eye on the place. You'll have to park on top of the cliff, or you'll be in a radio shadow, a blind spot.'

'I can bring the bike back in it too,' said Constable

Zeal. 'I pushed it so far and then abandoned it.'

'Aye, do that,' said Sergeant Lowes. 'You don't want to mistreat them, they'll take over one day. I should think on a bicycle all the brain is in the inner tubes; that's the bit to watch.'

'The pedals are the cranky bit,' said Constable Zeal.

*　　*　　*

'It's not like a police statement,' said David. 'I don't have to say it might be used in evidence, though I think it could be used. But your story is so strange that it must be true.'

'Of course it be true,' said Mr Babbacombe. 'Though I never saw it, only Martin did. But there isn't no other way round for it to have been, I fancy.'

'Well, I think it's clear,' said David, folding the complete claim form. 'Of course it has to go to Head Office, but they'll go by my report.' He had no doubt, now that he had spoken to Martin, and stood where he had stood, that the cows had been lost in the Swallow. 'They might send someone down to look in the Swallow,' he said. 'A diver.'

'Not wise,' said Mr Babbacombe. 'Never. They pools be safe for the most part if so be folk keep out of them. I recall long ago there was a little boat on the big one. And something come up one night and crushed it, smashed it quite up, and devoured part of it. There were pieces rising for weeks. Well, I know I throwed that damned policeman in, aggravating me with his statements, I shan't get money from they folk, but I reckon whatever it was in the Swallow have had its meat for the time and maybe won't be back for a

81

hundred years or so, that's how they go.'

David had had to content himself with smiling at
Jane when he could and when she was looking his way.
She had taken an interest in the claim form, and had
helped by naming and numbering the lost cows and
finding them in the herd book and knowing what they
had cost and their milk-yield history. But when the
form was filled it seemed that the visit was over. Mr
Babbacombe sat back in his chair beside the lowered
fire. Martin went on with his reading. David stood up.
No one offered to see him to the door. He gathered
up his papers until he had no hands left to do anything
with, and asked Jane if she would open the door. She
opened the door for him, and he went out. 'There's
my car door,' he said. 'If you could open that too.' So
he got her outside, and his voice dried in his throat.

'What are you doing tomorrow night?' he asked.

'Ironing, I think,' she said. 'If we get the electricity
back. They came today and weren't best pleased. The
posts all came loose one way and another.'

'I wondered if I could take you out,' said David.

'Oh, I don't know about that,' said Jane. 'No, I
don't. But I should like to see you again if you wanted
to come here. You've been kind to us, and there isn't
many that are.'

And then, for proof of her words, a stone came fly-
ing down from the white cliff above them and thudded
on the car.

David shouted at once, to hey, stop that. There was
a bright light on the cliff, and a notice lit up on a car
or van saying 'Police' and there were some shouts. Then
Constable Zeal came driving gently down the cliff road
and to the farm.

'You'd better go on inside, Miss,' he said. 'If you're

82

going now, Sir, I'll see you up into the fields. I'll stay here until all is quiet.'

'Oh no,' said David. 'I'll stay. You must remember that this farm is insured by Clandestine, and I am Clandestine's agent, and I ought to look after the company's interests.'

'All right,' said Constable Zeal. 'You stay here and give me a shout if anything happens. I'll be on the cliff and I'll get help if I need it. I have a couple of cracked ribs myself just now, or I'd be more useful. But, like you, Sir, it's better to prevent trouble than try to patch it up later. So if you can ignore provocation that will be best.'

10

Mr Babbacombe snored on. The candle flame stood still, with an occasional fidget. The fire crouched hidden under a layer of ash. David saw that Jane, like some human, sweated a little. He touched his own brow and felt moisture slip from skin to finger. Martin turned a page and studied the top line of the next one for a long time.

'You don't have to wait,' said Jane. 'There's no call for anything like that. We've had nastiness before, Mr Hayman, and *we* can get out, and *he*' (she meant Constable Zeal) 'can send for help. Last night Dad peppered two boys, nearly, and if they come again he'll salt them. We aren't afraid of folk; we aren't afraid of a worse thing there is in this house.'

David waited to hear what she said next. Martin's head fell forward on to the book. Jane reached forward and pulled the candle a little further from his head.

'They don't need this,' she said. 'We might go in the parlour with it.'

David let himself be taken through. They sat with the candle between them, at a small table. The air and

84

light in the room stopped, it seemed, at window and door, and all beyond was some dark medium, invisible, unseeing, unbreathable, solid. This capsule of parlour and the module of kitchen were all in the present space.

'What worse thing?' said David, fingering the warm wax below the candle flame.

'I won't believe it,' said Jane. 'I won't. It must be the blood in my ears. But they wouldn't hear it too, would they, Martin and Dad, and maybe Mr Zeal, but he wouldn't let on that he had, but I could see.'

Her hand came up and touched the other side of the candle, taking a solid drip from its column and feeding it in to the flame. The rich diet made the flame smoke.

'What was it?' said David. 'I can't hear anything.'

'Not now,' said Jane. 'But last night, and the night before.' She looked at him. There was flame in either eye, from the candle. David could not tell which way up the images were.

'Jane, tell me what it was,' said David. His finger slipped to her half of the candle shaft and touched one of hers.

'Don't burn me,' she said, tensing her hand and moving it a little out of range. David kept still. 'It's ghosts,' she said. 'Haunting. It's happened before, I've heard it before, but not so badly. They come running through the house.'

'People?' said David, 'apparitions?'

'They're not there to see,' said Jane. 'First they fight to get through the wall down in the kitchen. That wall.' And she indicated a wall not ten feet away, bringing the concept of the ghosts to within that distance. 'Then they parade down the house, so fast and loud, like, like Demons.'

Her hand trembled and David put his across to catch it. But there was a loud cry from outside and something struck his hand, his hand struck the candle, and there was darkness.

'Keep still,' he said in a whisper. 'Is that a demon?'

'No,' said Jane. Her seeking hand caught his. 'Not that sort. These are from the harbourside. Did you hear what they shouted?'

'Sorceress,' said Jane. 'That's what.'

'It's wicked,' said David.

' 'Tis nothing,' said Jane. 'They always called me that at school if they were against me sometimes. You can't choose what to learn but they think it's to do with mischief.'

'Don't stand in front of the window,' said David.

'Find the candle, Mr Hayman,' said Jane.

'My dear girl,' said David, 'in spite of the unpropitious circumstances I should be obliged and delighted if you would call me David.'

'That's high-up talk,' said Jane. 'Do you often speak like that?'

'Yes,' said David. 'It's a bad habit. But I meant to say, call me David, dear Jane.'

She squeezed his hand. He knelt down and crawled on the floor for the candle, finding it near the coal scuttle. By now his eyes were used to the deep dusk and he could see the window framing the night, and Jane standing by the kitchen door. He saw as well another figure by the window but outside. He came up to the window his side, sure he was invisible. His nose told him that the man outside was a fisherman. He found the range and got himself ready. The man played David's game, and came a foot nearer. David hit him in the belly and tried to hit him on the chin too, but struck air. Then he pulled the window down.

'Ignore provocation,' said Jane. 'Now you'll have set them going. We've had a stone or two in here before.'

86

'I could go out to the car and call up the policeman,' said David. 'But I don't like to step outside. I think we ought to shut all the windows and doors. Can they get in upstairs?'

'If they've a mind,' said Jane. 'But if we leave the windows open they likely won't break them.' David said they probably wouldn't anyway, but there was a clatter from the window he had just shut, and through the falling glass another stone hit the table.

The noise woke Mr Babbacombe. 'What's toward?' he said. 'Where's the candle, get that candle lit, maid, and be sharp,' and he was hunting in the cupboard among the rising shadows of David's lit match.

'Now stop him, Mr Hayman,' said Jane. 'David.'

'Who have you there behind my back?' said Mr Babbacombe. David heard the click of the gun being broken and loaded and put together again.

'Your friendly insurance man,' said David, stepping across and taking the gun. Mr Babbacombe had loaded it while he was more or less asleep, and was not ready for sudden action.

'Now behave yourself,' he said. 'You don't know what nonsense you're up to. They might have twenty guns out there, but I don't reckon they'll fire first.'

'I fired first yesterday,' said Mr Babbacombe. 'And I'm in the right, I be defending my own property, trespassers can look out or get out, no concern of mine they aren't, uninvited they are, unwanted.'

'Uninsured too,' said David.

'Sit down, father,' said Jane.

'You won't speak to me like that, Jane,' said Mr Babbacombe. 'I ain't to be ordered by no pert maid like you. I'll do as I fancy, as I think good.' He sat down.

There began outside, or perhaps in the house, a

strange sound. A continuous bouncing thudding, not very regular, began to be heard. Accompanying it and starting a few seconds later was a rustling in the garden.

'Damn it for some electric,' said Mr Babbacombe, but he was pushed down and told to keep quiet by Jane.

'They're throwing stones on to the roof,' said Martin. 'I know the sound; we've done it down in the town. You can't throw great rocks, just pebbles and they skitter about and plump down again, but they'd break your head if you got under them, dropping off the gutters. Go on, give them a shot, Mr Hayman.'

A clear pale light slanted across the room, touched here and there, and went out at the window again.

'That's the end of them,' said Mr Babbacombe.

'What do you mean?' said David. A remark so emphatic, short and decided made him uneasy. What had the farmer brought about that would rid him of the visitors? Would he have done less harm with his gun? Was there some craft that David knew nothing of, that the Babbacombes were skilled in, some power he was able to invoke? He looked at Jane for help, but she was staring too. He could not tell whether it was with the same curious wonder as his, or whether she had some knowledge that made her understand the full darkness of what had been said.

There was distant rumble of thunder. 'There,' said Mr Babbacombe. 'They'll not stop long in that.'

A few seconds later the candle went out again, when a draught of cold air swelled through the room, bringing with it a thickening of the atmosphere and a temporary swirl of mist. After this gale there was a multitude of little reports outside, as if pop-guns were being exploded by the diminutive soldiers of some dwarf army. The stones stopped falling on the roof.

'There,' said Mr Babbacombe, bending forward and stirring the fire. 'I said so, didn't I?' and he settled back in his chair and closed his eyes. David was lighting the candle with a match cupped in his hands. A door slammed shut upstairs.

'Rain,' said Martin. 'Thunderstorm.' The tiny explosive noises outside were the first huge drops falling in yard and garden. After them came a deluge, an unbreaking flood, and a change and change again of air in the room. The smoke of the fire was pulled up the chimney once more, but falling water splashed down bringing a cindery smell and spattering ash. Jane put the kettle on the fire, to keep the fire dry, as much as anything. The fire burnt underneath it, but round it the coal clinkered and darkened. The thunder rambled overhead and the lightning came from all sides. David went to the door, opened it, and looked out. A coming flash showed him the yard empty of people, his car standing axle-deep in rising spray. He could go now, he thought, but it was easy to disguise the fact from himself. He found he was hungry, and that the Babbacombe family evidently was too. Jane was setting the table, and the kettle was boiling.

'You'm welcome,' she said. 'I mean, you're welcome, David, if so be you wish to stay for what we have.'

'It so be I do,' said David. 'I mean, considering the external inclemency and the late hour I should be obliged by anything nourishing.'

Half an hour later they had all eaten substantially of cold meat and bread, a cherry pie, and a harvest cake that should not have been started yet but there was little else, Jane said. The rain began to lessen, and the thunder went out to sea and skirted the coast. Martin went out to look once and said it was blitzing Marret. 'They'll know we sent it,' he said.

Then, in the fresh calm after the storm, while David was letting his hand dangle beside his chair next to Jane's, the noises began once more. Jane heard them before David. He first noticed her forearm tensing, and then he felt the hair rising on it. Then, above the drip from the eaves or the heavy breathing of Mr Babbacombe asleep once more, there came a ticking in the wall, and then the thudding, and at last the pounding as if the wall would be broken through.

David stood up, because to sit still was unthinkable. He walked to the wall and touched it, and felt it thrilling and vibrating under his fingers. He lifted three cups from the dresser and set them on the table. Then there were two sharp raps, a short silence, and an example of the running noise through the house, not followed this time by the falling. What followed was more terrifying.

A screaming began under the floor, as if one lost soul were expiating its life of sin in Hell. Scream after scream came up, and the noise was unendurable, the thoughts the noise brought were unendurable, and the expectation of worse to come sent them all out of the house into the yard.

'No, I can't bear that,' said Mr Babbacombe. 'I can't bear that. They've returned, they've come back; they never were easy.'

'Who?' said David, thinking first of cows, though he had not heard such cries from cows or any beasts or any living thing.

'Those that we buried yonder,' said Mr Babbacombe. 'But nothing will take me there in the night now, no, nothing.'

'I'll take you into Marret,' said David. 'Or anywhere you like. You can't stay here.'

'We will,' said Mr Babbacombe. 'The barn by the shippon have all this year's hay in it still, and we can

90

lie warm there out of the way, and light ourselves out of the tractor battery.'

Away from the house the screams could not be heard. In the shippon and its adjoining barn there was a comfortable clean dryness and a steady atmosphere. David reflected that it was more luxurious and easy out here, and felt cleaner.

Mr Babbacombe turned on the tractor lights and did something with wires. He had a lamp lighting a corner of the hay, complete with a primitive switch, a pair of pliers connected to the wire and resting on another lump of farm metal. To switch off you lifted the pliers off the metal and let them hang. When he was satisfied with the device he burrowed into the hay and went to sleep. Martin found himself a place with his back to something and lay there looking at the roof.

Jane walked to the shippon door with David. He held two of her fingers; not yet her whole hand.

'Jane,' he said. 'I think I love you.' She made no comment either with word or gesture. 'Tell me about the cows. I will tell my company they should pay, because that is the evidence I have. But that is really because they could not refuse to pay. I would like to know for my own sake whether what they say happened is true.'

'Yes, it is true,' said Jane. 'And you are right to ask.'

'Tomorrow,' said David, beginning a sentence.

'Be tomorrow,' she said, slipping her hand away and running back across the concrete floor of the shippon, in and out of shadow.

David walked to his car and drove away.

11

After the storm the weather changed. The stillness went and a westerly wind brought a fresh coolness and more rain. It rained all night, then let the sun rise clear, and covered it before it had come far, and now there came occasional showers.

For Sergeant Lowes it was a calm digestive morning too, and he considered that he had learnt that the best breakfast was eggs, scrambled in plenty of milk. He had never had anything so quiet. He beamed on the town, in place of the absent sun. His benevolent attitude left no shadows. Why should one think, he mused, that any percentage of the population should be engaged in active crime. There would be accidental mis-behaviours from time to time, but everybody, surely, felt so much at peace with the world that passing annoyances could be disregarded.

Constable Zeal came in. Here was a man, thought the Sergeant, who disregarded passing annoyances, even when they seemed to be bringing him to the brink of death. Constable Zeal limped in, body bent, eyes dull, expression vacant.

'Ribs aching, eh?' said Sergeant Lowes, his bene-volence extending to sympathetic pity.

'Pleurisy, I wouldn't wonder,' said Constable Zeal. 'I've just got back.'

'You should have come in when it began to rain,' said Sergeant Lowes. 'Used your discretion. Any troublemakers went home when it began to rain.'

'Tried to,' said Constable Zeal. 'But the van wouldn't start. And there's nothing to report.'

'You should have radio'd back,' said Sergeant Lowes. 'We could have sent someone along.'

'You'll see how it is,' said Constable Zeal. 'I went down there and took up a position on the cliff and established radio contact with headquarters. It was obvious to me that people from the town were lurking about, and I asked them at the farm to take no notice of provocation, and to inform me by a pre-arranged signal if they needed help. Then I waited at the top of the cliff. There was, however, no disturbance, as far as I could tell. A visitor at the farm, the man from the insurance company, left after the thunderstorm. I then listened, and heard nothing, but thought it best to go down the hill and see that all was well. Accordingly I let the van free-wheel down the cliff road, and to the farm yard. I may say that the road is very much damaged by subsidence and surface water. Arriving at the farm I proceeded to look around. I found the farm unlocked and went in to see whether all was well. Apart from a low moaning sound, which I could not identify or locate, and the fact that no one was in the building, and a window was broken and that a recent meal had not been entirely cleared away, nothing seemed amiss. I was, however, uneasy, and proceeded to the van to make a call to you, Sergeant, and ask your advice. However, with the van being down below the cliff I was unable to make contact. The engine then would not start. I endeavoured to walk to the top of the cliff and

93

make my way to the road, but not feeling very well at the time I got into the van and closed my eyes. I then woke to find it was daylight and that Mr Babbacombe was at the door asking me what I was doing there. He was somewhat angry, but calmed down on being told of my orders. He consented to pull the van with his tractor until it started, and I have come straight here to report.'

'Right,' said Sergeant Lowes. 'I've been sitting here long enough. I'll take you home in my car, go to my own house for a sandwich, and take over the Babbacombe affair from you. You aren't fit to be on duty.'

Mr Babbacombe was busy with the tractor, filling in a gap in the road at the bottom of the cliff. He brought loads of white chalk to the trench that was forming there, and rammed the lumps down with the weight of the tractor. Sergeant Lowes bumped over the mend, and stopped in the yard with white tyres.

'Now, where did you spend the night?' he asked, when both men had looked at each other for some time, each knowing well who the other was but not wanting to speak without gathering all the new information possible.

'In the tallet,' said Mr Babbacombe. 'On the hay. We had the bogeys in last night, see.'

'Where from?' said Sergeant Lowes, thinking that Mr Babbacombe meant 'policemen' for 'bogeys'.

'Hell,' said Mr Babbacombe. 'That's where, isn't it?'

'Reasonable,' said Sergeant Lowes. 'But wasn't it folk from the town paying a visit?'

'Not that wasn't,' said Mr Babbacombe. 'No, that were our own old folk returning, I knew the voices of many of them.'

'I don't reckon I'm with you,' said Sergeant Lowes.

'Ah,' said Mr Babbacombe, and he drove away on

94

the tractor to scoop up another load of chalk. Sergeant Lowes interpreted his last remark, 'Ah' as meaning that he would expand further at a suitable moment, but was busy now. Sergeant Lowes spent the time looking at the Swallows.

He saw three level innocent pools, reflecting more light, as sometimes happens, than they seemed to receive. Sergeant Lowes knew about their consistent level, that they did not fill at flood or fall at drought. His eye went round the edge of the water and saw that above the water there was grass and green land stuff, and below it water stuff and plain mud. The line of change was exactly at the water level.

He walked from the large pool to the next one, and the same applied there. He looked back at the big one. Something was different from this angle. At the far side, now, where he had been standing before, the water level and the change of vegetation did not coincide any more. There was a long crescent of muddy ground showing. There were small creatures moving on the brown beach exposed. His eyes went round and found an explanation. The ground had tipped, and the water level dropped a little, so that at one side the original level was the same, and at the other it was lower. He peered over the edge of the second pool, which was nearest to him, and found there were little crabs in the mud. And something else that moved was a small flat fish, a dab.

Mr Babbacombe finished his filling of the trench, turned off the tractor engine, and came to Sergeant Lowes.

'Now,' he said, 'I admit it, but I'm a rough man and I was out of humour like, and on my own land, and it be his word against mine.'

'Constable Zeal?' said Sergeant Lowes. 'You weren't

yourself, Black Babbacombe, or you wouldn't have done it.'

'No,' said Mr Babbacombe, 'I wouldn't; I'd have broke him.'

'Never mind about that,' said Sergeant Lowes. 'Tell me about these Swallows.'

'It was the big one where it happened,' said Mr Babbacombe. 'But I didn't see it.'

'Did anyone?' said Sergeant Lowes. 'Well, wouldn't the thought pass your mind?'

'Yes, directly,' said Mr Babbacombe. 'And Martin, he saw it, and didn't credit it enough to tell me. They say there's something terrible about these Swallows, and they've always said it.'

'They've shifted,' said Sergeant Lowes. 'When did they do that?'

'Bound to have shifted,' said Mr Babbacombe. 'You see that crack in the road I filled just now? Well, that crack will open again tonight. The land's slipping away here, and these Swallows are slipping with it. That'll be a pity, if anything comes to them; they're good clear sweet water, none better. You could taste it now, there've been no cows for a day or two, and no creatures neither. 'Tis the time of doom, when the creatures go, 'tis a sign, and when the dead rise and walk and talk, then 'tis for sure.'

'Tell me about that,' said Sergeant Lowes. 'I've not been to your cemetery. It's out on the cliffs, isn't it?' He creaked his knees down and dipped his scooping hand into the water, lifted the water up and tasted it. He was not surprised to find it tasted salty. 'Try some yourself,' he said. 'I think it's a bit off today.'

'This land came out of the sea,' said Mr Babbacombe. 'And one day the sea will come back for it, that's what they said. But I say it stands to reason that can't be so, such a great piece of land as this.' He tasted the water himself, and spat. 'Well, then,' he said. 'That's only more of the same. The sea is rising up and taking it back, and those be little sea creatures come up with the water, harbingers, that's what.'

'I can't reckon it out,' said Sergeant Lowes. 'Here we are thirty or forty feet above sea level. How can it be sea water?'

'How can it have taken nine cows?' said Mr Babbacombe.

'Beats me,' said Sergeant Lowes. 'But what about last night and the ancestors walking? That was just towns-folk, surely?'

'No,' said Mr Babbacombe. 'They weren't *seen*, they walked invisible, under the ground, about the house. It was more than we could stand, and we were driven out. But we're back in by daylight, and there's just a whimper now and then.'

'Trickery,' said Sergeant Lowes. 'I'd better come and listen.'

Mr Babbacombe took him to the house. He listened, and there was a faint trundling noise to be heard within the walls, or perhaps under the floor.

'It's the drains,' said Sergeant Lowes. 'Depend on it.'

'Not very likely,' said Mr Babbacombe. 'There isn't a drain in the place except for the shippon.'

'Is the house still upright?' said the Sergeant. 'Have you checked it? Will it fall in on you?'

'Eggs don't roll off the table yet,' said Jane. 'And the pictures don't cling nor swing out, so it must be straight up.'

'Well I'm going out of it,' said Sergeant Lowes. 'Black Babbacombe, take me to the cemetery. I'm going to have a good look round now I'm here. I've brought my dinner and I'll eat it out there and continue my researches.'

'They're all up and walking,' said Mr Babbacombe.

The cemetery was two fields away, at the edge of the cliff. The chapel that once went with it had gone down the cliff by itself. It seemed that the cemetery would once more be with it in a little while, because more ground had fallen. Sergeant Lowes and Mr Babbacombe walked to the edge with care.

Down below them lay the broken cliff of a fall, with the sea still busy and staining itself taking the fresh soil.

'Not so long down, that,' said Mr Babbacombe. 'And there, see, is great aunt Elizabeth.'

Sergeant Lowes expected a living person still, perhaps walking over the ground. But Mr Babbacombe was pointing down the cliff at something a little lighter than the slope it lay on. There was a bone, and another bone, hip and shoulder, and there was the round great seedpod of a human skull, dormant in the same earth.

'She was just here,' said Mr Babbacombe. 'She have broken out again, same as I always knew she would.' They came to her headstone, which would be the next thing to go: half its width jutted out over the water. *Elizabeth Babbacombe,* said the writing, *I am not dead, saith the Lord.* Mr Babbacombe hopped over the edge of the cliff, scrabbled about for a little while to gain a footing, went a little way, and came back with the skull.

'Her thinking-piece,' he said. 'She would outwit me many a time, and I owe her respect. You know, Mr Lowes, we live our own way here, not just regardless of the whole world. We'm no worse than your ordinary cat, that doesn't obey a rule at all, but it lives a moral life; well, so do we here, and here we've been, Babbacombes and,' here he laid his hand on another tomb-stone. 'Blacks, these many years.' *Robert Black*, said this stone *My people shall be gathered unto me.*

'I thought you were all atheists,' said Sergeant Lowes. 'But these inscriptions are out of the Bible.'

'Maybe,' said Mr Babbacombe. 'But they mean the sea, not anyone else. 'Tis the sea will come back.'

Then they came to where the ground had opened, a wide crack three feet across, and darkly deep so that no bottom could be seen. Here Mr Babbacombe was able to take another skull and the bones of a leg. The owner had been *Babbacombe Black, Haste ye to me.* Sergeant Lowes went to the land side of the crack, and said he would have his lunch. Mr Babbacombe went back to the house with his two forebears, the crop of this strange field. Sergeant Lowes wondered if he had a cupboard full of them.

He found a fallen stone and spread on it the plastic bag his wife had put round the lunch box. He decided it would not rain for a while.

He opened the plastic box. Mrs Lowes had done well for him and provided the leg of a chicken, bread and butter, a tomato, a square of cake, and a piece of cheese. He had a flask of cold tea in another pocket. 'Picnic,' he said to himself. 'A treat, this,' and he ate the chicken down to the bone. He was disconcerted to find that he had produced this part of a skeleton himself. It seemed an unmannerly thing to do, pointing out morta-lity to those no longer with it. It would have been easy to sit in the next field, fifty feet away, and offend no one, living or dead. He dropped the bone into the crack in the ground, using it as a guide to the depth of the fissure.

He did not hear it fall, for certain. There was a soft sort of noise, that was all. He thought there would be nothing else. But a moment later there was a violent bellowing roar down below, as if he had woken a primeval Babbacombe. After the roar, which was startling and unnerving enough, there came a fearsome hellish belch of the most disgusting and repelling kind, like the decay of a century. Sergeant Lowes hurried to his feet and ran away. He had managed the first slight revulsion of having chewed on bone among the bones of the dead, but this was too much for a stomach that habitually sent out delicate messages of surfeit. He was sick over the edge of the cliff.

*   *   *

David came down to the farm late in the afternoon. His work was done for the day. He left the car at the top of the cliff, because it was now raining and he knew the track was slippery in the wet. He put on his coat and walked down to the farm.

There was no answer when he knocked at the door. He left it and went to the shippon. Here it was obvious that the tractor had been moved, and indeed was still slightly warm. He thought that meant the family had been about, and had passed the night quietly, even if not comfortably.

He went back to the house. There was still no reply. He pushed the door and it opened. That was nothing out of the way for him to do: in country districts the best way of being noticed was to open the door and shout. He shouted. There was no reply. He stepped inside. There was no one in the kitchen. No one recent, that is. But two skulls looked at him from the table, and beside them two brown mimic eggs.

12

Martin spent the day hidden either in the coverts of lessons or the less concealing structures of the school cloakrooms. He had come to school with hay in his clothes and the hay had been the subject of enquiry, except, particularly, from Stinking Tom and Pewter and one or two others who benefited from being drawn along in their fringe. They were the outcast mob of the school, and Martin often felt that he was numbered among them. They were usually part of his accustomed shelter, but today he wanted to shelter even from them. At moments towards the end of breaks and the dinner hour he ran across the school yard and looked out towards the farm. On one of these occasions, running in, he heard from a smaller pupil that he stank nearly as much as Stinking Tom. He smelt his jacket, and knew that he smelt like his father.

He had been to look across the water at the farm because the doom-laden feeling he had could only be vanquished by a greater feeling of satisfaction when something happened there. He did not know what the happening could be, but it would be, he was sure. When he came in after dinner from the swift observing, his jacket was wet from a shower that passed over. From the window of the science lab, high up in the school, he saw the shower move over the water and obscure the farm and its headland. He hoped, in some way, that they would not come to his sight again; perhaps when the screening rain went there would be nothing beyond but clean clear sea.

He knew that fantasies like that were only a form of excitement, and meant nothing, but the image of a clear sea stayed with him all the afternoon, and became part of his camouflage, so that in his shrubbery of events, his woodland of timetable, he was more hid than ever.

When he came out of school he was met by Jane. He supposed for a time that something had happened. She was searching the common background of rather similar boys for him, thinking that all looked alike. It was his best concealment of the day. He had to walk up to her and take off his cap (against school rules to go bare-headed, but with them to raise the cap to a lady) before she knew him.

Nothing had happened, she said. Mr Babbacombe had realized that there was nothing to do at the farm tonight, and had come into Marret with Jane for a change. They were to have a meal out together, and then be escorted home by Sergeant Lowes.

'I take it kindly of him,' said Mr Babbacombe, when they were drinking tea at a café, and the rain was pouring down outside the window and the day under this new shower was like the dusks of winter. 'But I think he have a scheme to dis-lodge us out of our own house and place us somewhere, like getting the Parish or some council to say our own house en't no more safe, which it is, of course, that tipping land be the other side, and what's a bit of crumble near the cliffs? I reckon we might be in for trouble with them old ancestors shifting about, but that en't a danger.'

'If that was ancestors then let's go to the workhouse,' said Martin. 'I've heard of workhouses; they give you a Christmas dinner, time it comes round.'

'I was frightened,' said Jane.

'I was terrified,' said Mr Babbacombe. 'I knowed some of them when I was a boy, like great aunt Elizabeth. We'm well away in the shippon; they used to live regular among their beasts in the olden days, no trouble to them it wasn't, and if it was, why, we have no beasts now, who's to object?'

'I don't want to go back,' said Martin. 'But I won't do anything about it. I just feel that I never shall be back there, and I'm glad of it.'

'Now cheer yourself,' said Mr Babbacombe. 'Have one of they jam doughnuts at the counter there, go on, boy, that'll set you right-side up.'

The jam doughnut settled itself the wrong side up when it had been swallowed. Martin still felt unconvinced about the probability of returning to Swallow Farm.

'You've been listening too much to father and his dooms,' said Jane. 'Why don't you have a jam doughnut too, Dad, and be settled too?'

'No,' said Mr Babbacombe. 'That's the boy's treat.'

The boy and his treat felt slightly unwell, between them.

* * *

'Uncommon nasty,' said Sergeant Lowes, who had called in a friendly, informative way on Constable Zeal. Constable Zeal was knitting the thumb on to a mitten

for his daughter in her pram. 'Uncommon nasty,' said
Sergeant Lowes. 'Sitting in a damp graveyard, and out
of the ground comes this stench, sickened me it did.
Then near killed me, I don't know what that ground
opens up to, but I can guess.'

'It isn't many that believe in the actual existence of
Hell,' said Constable Zeal.

'One person does from now,' said Sergeant Lowes.
'Or he knows what it'll be like if it does exist. It was
my duty to investigate so I came back to this crack in
the ground and looked down, holding my breath. I
could smell it through my held breath, how's that for
a smell?'

'Heavy, I'd say,' said Constable Zeal. 'I'd be obliged
if you would pass that darning needle and save me the
pain of getting up, Sergeant.'

'Pleased,' said the Sergeant, rolling his finger ends
round it and bringing to Constable Zeal. 'The only
method of investigation that suggested itself was visual,
at that time. I dropped a lighted match down the
chasm.'

'What did you see?' said Constable Zeal. 'Now, is
that the right thumb or the left one?'

'I didn't see so much,' said the Sergeant. 'The bloody
thing blew up in my face, like dropping matches in
petrol, crack, it went up, bowled me over, I can tell
you. Then it began to pour with rain, so I went back
to the farmhouse.'

'It all hangs together,' said Constable Zeal, holding
up the mitten he was working on.

'It won't matter if it doesn't,' said Sergeant Lowes.
'She can't tell at her age.'

'I don't mean the mitten,' said Constable Zeal. 'I
mean the tale about the cows and what happened to
you.'

'No,' said Sergeant Lowes. 'One and one make two, and two and two make four, Constable. All we've got is one, he says some cows are lost, two, he might make a claim for them. I suppose you could add, three, he tried to drown you, and four, he tried to blow me up, but he couldn't have planned that.'

'Ah, that's composition,' said Constable Zeal. 'But I was thinking of decomposition, like the gases in the stomach of a cow, or stomachs, since a cow has four.'

'They have four of everything,' said Sergeant Lowes. 'But I'm glad I've one stomach only, and sometimes I think that's decomposed enough.'

'I'll tell you my line of thought,' said Constable Zeal. 'If it is true that the cows went down ino the pool, then they went somewhere. It seems to me that there must be a way down through the ground towards the sea, because that's where the water will drain to. So, somewhere between the pool and the sea is where the cows are, and why not under this cemetery of yours?'

'Not mine, quite,' said Sergeant Lowes. 'But I thought it was when that thing blew up. I thought they'd been smuggling high explosive.'

'A dead cow decomposes,' said Constable Zeal. 'Like all dead bodies. After some days the belly is distended with gases. I suppose the skin broke and released these gases, accounting for the smell, and since these gases are combustible, accounting for the explosion.'

'You mean I'd better not smoke between meals?' said Sergeant Lowes. 'On account of belches?'

'I expect you can carry on until you've been dead some days,' said Constable Zeal.

'I'm comforted,' said Sergeant Lowes. 'Now I'm going back with the Babbacombe family to settle them in the shippon for the night. I want them to leave, because the place isn't safe, none of it. There's going to be a big settlement there one of these days, and I'd like them out soon.'

He called at the station before going down to the bus station for the Babbacombes. Before he left Constable Zeal he had quite dismissed the theory about cows, without adding an explanation to the facts in its place. Really he thought that Black Babbacombe had committed a fraud and would not be found out. Sergeant Lowes smiled at the thought: without minding much about the crime, he looked forward to being able to prove it had happened; he could in that way enjoy it twice.

At the station the message he received made his conviction a little less secure. A large dead animal had been discovered floating just outside the harbour, and a fishing boat was now bringing it in. Some reports said it was a whale, others that it was an albatross of enormous dimensions, and a third suggested it was a cow.

'It will be,' said Sergeant Lowes, feeling a traitor to his own senses. 'I'm sorry to say.' But it need not be a Babbacombe cow, and it need not have been through the Swallow: it would not be beyond Black Babbacombe to have pushed it straight over the cliff.

Sergeant Lowes went down to the harbour. The fishing boat had come in with a dark bulk hauled behind it. It tied up at the wooden jetty, and lights were shone on its tow.

It was a cow, floating on its back, with distended belly, legs apparently out of scale, and udder diminished too by reason of the large size of the abdomen.

'Right you lads, easy with her,' said Sergeant Lowes. 'I think I can get it identified.'

But some excited onlooker, very likely Stinking Tom, climbing among the wooden supports of the jetty, had jabbed at the corpse with a hook and pierced the skin.

Sergeant Lowes for the second time that day felt the stink of hell rise round him. This time he managed to keep his stomach under control, while at the same time regretting that Constable Zeal could probably be right.

The boy who was pulled out of the water after falling in from the woodwork below was Stinking Tom. He went home, retching. The cow sank low in the water.

The Sergeant knew what to do, though. 'One of you down there, cut off its left ear,' he said. 'Look sharp, before you lose it altogether. No, don't argue with me, son; this is the Police.'

In due course an ear was handed to the Sergeant.

'Olé,' said someone.

'That's the second I've fought today,' said the Sergeant. Then he hurried off with his prize to the bus station.

'Now, Mr Babbacombe,' he said. 'Did you lose a brown cow?'

'Nothing else,' said Mr Babbacombe.

'And what's your herd number?'

'479,' said Mr Babbacombe. 'BST, that's for Barsetshire, 479.'

'We've had one of your cows in the harbour,' he said. 'Bit dark to see, but I got the ear off it and it's a brown one, and the tag on it has your number, so I reckon that proves it, don't you?'

'A brown cow is a brown cow, but for the number,' said Mr Babbacombe. 'They're not quite up to being as different as people, but they're well enough in their way.'

'I wouldn't mind ear-tagging some folk,' said Sergeant Lowes. 'Do you mind if I keep this ear for a bit; we might need it for something or other. And now I'll run you all home.'

They went out into a night that was streaming and

got into a Police Car. Sergeant Lowes drove them home, and into their own yard.

'Sure you want to be here?' he said, as they went between the Swallows. 'We could fix you up in town.'

'The house isn't there,' said Martin. 'It can't be. It isn't reasonable.'

But it was there, and in the yard, in his car that he had at last brought down so that he could sit in it, was David.

'Is this trouble?' said Sergeant Lowes.

'No,' said Jane. 'It's a friend, and I've kept him waiting.'

'Advance and be identified, friend,' said Sergeant Lowes. 'I think we'll keep an eye on everybody here just now.'

David made himself known. Sergeant Lowes put on his cap and took a wet walk round the house, and looked inside as well. Then he took his car up to the top of the cliff and walked down again.

'I'll sit in the house,' he said. 'Dark it may be, but I'll not be put out by any hauntings, because there's an explanation of them all.'

Martin, disappointed that the end of the day did not bring the final shelter of hope, or expectation fulfilled, went to bed again in the shippon. Mr Babbacombe, with nothing to keep him awake, went too. Sergeant Lowes came back from his car and entered the house. David and Jane went in with him.

'No lights, of course,' said Jane, flicking the switch idly.

The lights came on: the electricity had been reconnected. There was a note about it on the table.

'There, now it's easy for a cup of tea,' said Jane.

13

Martin had not come to rest, he found. The hay was hot, the barn oppressive, but for all that there was a quick cold wind blowing in on him through the wall. But he wanted to be close to the wall, to give his back something to be against, so that all approaches of danger should be from one direction only.

It was not dangers that made threats against him now. He had come back to Swallow Farm knowing that it would not be there. Either it would have fallen, or been burnt, or there would have been a decision on his father's part to stay away. But these ends to the thread of living had not been cut yet. He was back at the farm; it was still there; his father had not made any decision at all about anything.

It was this summer, Martin thought, that doubts had come to him. When he had been small a father had been a father, someone to help as seriously as possible about the farm's affairs. Later, at the new school, there had been a certain notoriety in being the son of Black Babbacombe, who was reputed to be one of the bad ones of the world, him and his parents and ancestors. At school though, they had given up expecting Martin to show the same conniving wickedness. They were disappointed in him, perhaps. But there was enough air of past misdeeds in the family for Martin to be classed with a certain lot of other pupils, somewhere on the lower edge of the acceptable. It was not the best place to be. It was no longer fun to have a reputation for a murky past or an unusual family. It was less bearable this year, too, because he had begun to see that his own immediate wicked ancestor was nothing of the sort; he was a fat, ageing farmer who was never very clean, who had no ambition beyond the hedge of his furthest field except to drink too much cider about once a month. In fact the alleged wickedness was dull, boring in quite a positive way, biting into all aspects of existence and spoiling it. Now, when things had happened, when cows had been lost spectacularly, when the house was surrounded by hostile villagers, when it was paced by intrusive ghostly noises, the best reaction of his father was to go to sleep, recoiling from the actuality as if he had been beaten into submission by it.

Martin lay waking. Mr Babbacombe slept. Martin wondered, not for the first time that year, what hope there could be. There was none for Jane, he thought. She would go on housekeeping, until she turned at last to Jemmy Hagblow, in a succession of sunless summers and bleak dark winters. Himself he saw trapped between the upper and the lower stones of the mill, with neither stone moving: even if the mill were not working, it might at least fall down and let the trapped life feel there were still forces like gravity.

The only force he felt now was the cold draught. And there was a glimmer of light coming across the shippon and making a molecular sort of mark on a beam above him. He fingered it, and brought it into the palm of his hand. Then he knelt up in his hay and looked down the shaft of light. It blackened his eye against seeing. He got right out of the straw and felt his way down the ladder and across the shippon.

The house lights were on. Suddenly he felt rested after his long course of thoughts, refreshed, as if he had come round new to a beginning. Or if that thought did not last him the journey across the yard, then the one that something might be going that would distract him was still there.

Nothing much distracted him. The kitchen door opened to him. He went in. Jane was tidying away some brown things that looked to his slightly dazzled eyes like skulls. The Policeman was at the sink turning a tap to get water to fill the kettle. The Insurance man was burning paper in the hearth, trying to light the fire.

'These won't be the taps, then, Miss Babbacombe,' said Sergeant Lowes. 'Not a drop comes from them.'

'Oh yes, they are,' said Jane. 'But that sometimes happens, the pipe blocks. Dad can dig it out in the morning. We can go out to the Swallows if you like, but if it's raining enough it'll fill at the rainspout off the roof.'

'This morning there was salt water in those pools,' said Sergeant Lowes. 'It stands to reason they connect with the sea some way or other. But that doesn't fill the kettle. Where's the best spout, young Martin?'

Martin knew where to fill the kettle. He stood in the rain while he did it. The smoke from the newly-started fire came down the side of the house on to him. Jane took it from him and plugged it in. David got up from the fire and had to go outside to clean his hands.

They drew the curtains and closed the door. The fire sprang up lively, the kettle boiled, and they had a cup of tea. Jane went out to the shippon with one for Mr Babbacombe, but he was asleep.

'Well now,' said Sergeant Lowes, when he had drunk his two cups. 'I reckon your alarms and excursions are over for the night.'

'They weren't by this time last night,' said David.

'That was a domestic affair,' said Sergeant Lowes. 'A family matter,' and he nodded towards the two skulls sitting in the bottom of the window with the curtains hooding them. 'I don't reckon there'll be anyone about outside tonight, and that's what I'm concerned with. Mind, I'm concerned about the whole safety of this place. I just have a feeling of danger, but nothing I can add up; there's no two and two in it.'

'The place has gone funny,' said Martin. 'It doesn't feel real any more.'

'It's time you were in your bed,' said Jane. 'You've done with your tea, go on up to your room.'

'I'll go to the shippon,' said Martin. But he was not able to argue with them when they said that the Sergeant and David would stay downstairs all night long. 'I'm not afraid,' he said. 'It isn't that. It doesn't feel right to be here any more, it's like being in school after hours.'

'Don't fancy things,' said Jane. 'A bit pixilated, you are. How could we be not meant to be here? It's our house and our land, and has been for ever back, and this Sergeant here represents the Queen, isn't that so, Mr Lowes?'

'Yes,' said Sergeant Lowes.

'So you'm just tired, midear,' said Jane. 'Get on with you to bed.'

Martin went upstairs, feeling that he was revisiting the house after a thousand years, when by some miracle nothing had happened to it.

'I think I'll be going back to the car,' said Sergeant Lowes. 'I'll stay up there a bit, then come down and have a look round, and maybe then I'll go.'

'I'll do the same as yesterday,' said David. 'If anything happens at all I'll come out and blow the horn
of my car and flash the lights.'

'I'll look out for both,' said the Sergeant. 'It's getting
to be a wild night, wind and rain coming.'

He went out.

'David,' said Jane, 'I've been thinking of you today.'

'I have been thinking of you, Jane,' said David. 'I
came here hours ago, and there was no one left here but
two skulls. I stayed in the car from half past four until
nine o'clock.'

'I didn't know what we were doing,' said Jane. 'I had
no idea. I went shopping in Marret, and Dad came too,
and then we stayed and stayed, and they found one of
the cows, that's a proof you want, isn't it?'

'It depends how you found it,' said David. 'Did the
same thing happen to them still?'

'It was in the sea,' said Jane. 'But, David, I don't
want you to go because I'm frightened for the night.
And I don't know whether you should stay, because
I've little enough you could have, nothing to offer you.'

'Why not?' said David.

'No, don't hold my hand,' said Jane. 'It wouldn't be
right to let you think you could. It might look possible
for us to be friends, but perhaps it's not even that. I
can't let you think of me at all, David. This is my place
here, and I've got my family to look after—not Martin
so much, because he'll find his own way, but Dad. I've
managed for him for seven years now, and I suppose
I'll manage for him a bit longer and then Jimmy Hagblow will bring his bit of land in with ours and they've
planned that I shall wed him, and move up to their
house and Martin have this one, and I'll still have Dad.
So you see my way is fixed for me, and I can't turn aside.

113

And Dad will get worse, I'm sure. They all have this fate on them, the Babbacombes and the Blacks, and they never fight against it. They own this land but they think it must be against them, and we never prosper. They hate us round about and they despise us for some of what they did in the old days, and because we've come down so from what there once was here. This down below the cliff was the worst bit of the Babbacombe and Black land, and now it's all they have left. Well, it's what I was born to, like the rest of the Babbacombes, and I can't fight it. They can't manage by themselves, and no one else would come and manage for them, and there's nothing to pay them with if they did come. We're still paying taxes on my grandmother's death.'

David sat and digested what she had said in silence. Jane herself touched the fire up with a falsely calm demeanour. But tears started from her eyes and she sobbed. Then David stood up and something like tears rose to his eyes. They stood for a moment on the hearthrug, either side of the fire, and then they were in each others' arms.

Jane pulled herself away in a little while. 'No,' she said. 'It's like Dad's doom, it's what's on me, it's what is bound to happen, and there's nothing we can do. I think that's all the happiness we can have, David, and you'll have to go away and forget me, and I'll stay here and forget you.'

'No,' said David. 'Not forget you.'

'At last you will,' said Jane. 'Perhaps not at once. But you'll see that my life doesn't lead to your life. My life only leads to where I'm going. I can't get free of it, I'm pixilated by it, I can't step aside, even if it isn't where I want to go.'

'I'll wait,' said David.

'There's nothing to wait for,' said Jane. 'It wouldn't be enough even if I loved you, and I'm not sure of that yet, or I am sure enough, perhaps, so that I can't allow it to be any more so. I shan't be unhappy, you know. I suppose I shall have children, but they won't be yours, and even so they will make me happy and make me grieve. No, David, there's nothing for us here, and we shall just have to bear it. Dad will go on being what he is, a farmer in a small way, and things might be better in with the Hagblows, if they don't fight too much. Perhaps my children will get away from the doom and the place. I stayed at school three years longer than Dad, and I know things he never heard of. But mine will stay until they have heard of things I know nothing about, and I won't let them stay near me.'

'Jane,' said David, hoping that if he started calmly and seriously he might be able to sort out what he meant to say in his turn. 'If it isn't enough to love each other...'

He was interrupted. Sergeant Lowes came in at the door, after having hurried through the rain.

'There's something rum up on the cliff,' he said. 'Will you come out and see? And what's the matter with the floor in here?'

They looked down at the floor. Water was rising, silently, between the flags, welling up and deepening.

14

There was wet inside the house. There was wet outside it too, and through it something came quickly, splatteringly, in an unhesitant approach. Then, grinning foolishly in the door, stood a dog, dancing on the spot he stood, tail moving gently but stowed away between his legs and under his belly.

'Robot,' said Jane. 'What a fright you gave us, then. Where've you been, then boy, where? I know, you been up at Jemmy's; what did you leave home for. Well, you shouldn't be in here, boy, so off you go to your own place. Bed now, boy.'

But Robot did not go. He danced on the same ground and grinned, all his teeth showing at one side, and whimpered.

Sergeant Lowes went towards him with an outstretched hand. Robot lunged forward and took him by the leg. Sergeant Lowes stepped back.

'That wasn't a bite,' he said. 'More like a remark. Is he safe to go by, though. I don't like the look of him.'

'I'll put him in his place,' said Jane. 'He could come in but he can't sit on this floor. Come on, Robot.'

Robot waited until she came to him and then started

to shepherd her out of the house by snapping at her ankles.

'He's a cow-dog,' said Jane. 'Mostly. Stop it, Robot, get down, boy.' She was trying to take no notice of his directions, but Robot was used to evasion, and was managing to move her away from the door and into the yard.

'No collar,' said Sergeant Lowes. 'What is there?' He saw a red scarf that Mr Babbacombe wore in winter and took that. He stepped up behind Robot, was bitten on the arm, and put the scarf round the dog's neck, then held him down firmly. Robot howled.

Jane said he might be best in the shippon; they could go there without her and she could get back into the house again. Sergeant Lowes and David put the dog in at the door and closed it on him, then came back to the house.

'We've to go on the cliff,' said Sergeant Lowes, as they splashed across the yard. Robot thumped on the door, howled once, and then was quiet. 'I'd rather take them all out of here at once,' said the Sergeant. 'There's something not right. I don't like that floor and the water on it. I don't like the cliff in the dark. I don't like sea-water in those pools. I don't like any of it very much, and least of all I like the way Black Babbacombe isn't taking any notice of the world, as if he knew the worst was to happen and wasn't going to do anything about it, like a fatalist he is, or some tribesman that's had a spell cast on him.'

In the kitchen Jane was putting more coal on the fire. The room was warm, comfortable, as the Ark must have been to Noah, the only place in the flood; though here the flood had entered into the sanctuary.

'Just looked in to say we're off out again,' said Sergeant Lowes. 'We got your dog Computer locked away.'

'Robot,' said Jane.

'Something like that,' said Sergeant Lowes. 'But I want this young man to come up and look on the cliff with me. If it's a trouble-maker he may have made trouble for himself, either by being caught by us, or by getting caught up on something.'

'You told Martin you would stay here all night,' said Jane.

'Neither of you need worry,' said David. 'Need they, Sergeant? We'll be down if you shout.'

'We can be down before that if we're not careful,' said Sergeant Lowes. 'But we aren't going climbing, just along the path at the top.'

They splashed away through the dark. Jane left the door open, and stood there watching Sergeant Lowes's hand-lamp and its searching clear on the cliff. From the shippon came the noise of Robot becoming excited about something.

They walked along the road and between the Swallows.

'Crabs in there,' said Sergeant Lowes. 'If not worse. That was salt water this morning.'

They climbed the road up the cliff, as far as the fence that protected the footpath. Here the wind lifted off the sea, paused on the lower land, and then went straight up the cliff before flattening again. Heads felt blown inland, and legs seemed sucked outwards in some vortex. Sergeant Lowes went first, shining the torch on the ground to pick up footprints.

'You look about,' he said. 'Don't look at the light, just stay close. I won't walk off the edge.'

They moved about twelve feet along the path. David saw the bulk of Sergeant Lowes stop, and stopped himself.

'Back, gently,' said Sergeant Lowes. 'Don't touch anything.' David backed, turning round slowly. The Sergeant followed, saying nothing until they reached the road again.

'Electricity pole,' he said. 'Stands on the cliff edge along there, supply to the house. It's slipped out, and the wires are about four feet above the path, you could put your hand on the insulators, and I bet they aren't insulating everything this weather. It's a wonder we didn't get into a wire down there. The path fell away too, or I might have gone straight into the wire.'

'Do you think there's anybody else about?' said David.

'Not for a minute,' said Sergeant Lowes. 'But I'll get them to close the far end. Only a fool would be on that path tonight, and fools are lucky.' He got into his car and spoke to the Police Station in Marret.

Then they walked down the track again, this time with their faces to the wind.

'Invigorating,' said Sergeant Lowes. 'I wish I was home in bed.'

David did not wish anything like that. He had no vision of any other world than the present actual one, unresolved, wet, unhappy, and holding no promises of future days.

In the shippon Robot was barking still and making a hysterical noise, as if he were responding to someone. Sergeant Lowes noticed that it was like speech. Then a light went on in the shippon and they knew that part of what they heard was speech and that Mr Babbacombe had been woken.

'Bitten him, no doubt,' said Sergeant Lowes. 'That's two that dog has had tonight apart from me.'

'Too late to insure you against that,' said David. It was too late to insure against anything, he thought. Or perhaps there is no comprehensive insurance against a complete rejection of a suit, against being told to go away before arrival. There is no premium payable to cover you against the risk of other people's thoughts and convictions.

Jane was still waiting in the doorway. But not for me, David knew. She was just waiting for any protection he offered; she was holding on to him because he was a point of light in the darkness, and Sergeant Lowes was another.

'It might have been February,' said Sergeant Lowes. 'There's that to be glad of.' He would have stepped across the room to the fire, but now there was more water underfoot indoors than there was outside. Outdoors perhaps it had somewhere to run. Here the skirting board kept it in.

'Won't it go through the house?' he said, stepping to the far door instead of to the fire. The door opened to the parlour. It resisted his push: water had already filled the parlour nine inches deep. A wave slopped across the kitchen and threw ashes out from below the fire. Fresh red cinder dropped through the grate and hissed.

'Get that boy out,' said Sergeant Lowes. 'I'll take her to the shippon.'

There was not much air of heroic rescue about what happened now. Sergeant Lowes and Jane walked calmly out of the house and across the yard. That should have been David's place in a right world, but this world was out of true. Instead he went up the stairs and found Martin lying asleep on his bed, with the light full on.

'Come out of the house,' said David, and, a sudden panic seizing him, he picked Martin up and carried him out of the room. Martin lay still until they were in the yard and David put him down.

'What's with the heavy rescue?' he said.

'I had to save somebody,' said David. 'You ought to be away from here: there isn't anything we can do.'

'I know,' said Martin. 'We shouldn't have come back. We should have left it all alone.'

'I don't know what you mean,' said David, though he knew that he well understood. 'It's the drains, that's all, flooding the house.'

They came to the shippon. Here the electric light was on. Robot had climbed the ladder to the hay and was tied there now. He had woken Mr Babbacombe, who had come down the ladder and was sitting on a milk can looking at the floor.

When he was asked he said he was all right, not ailing in any particular, just waiting for his time.

Robot howled a long howl, broke the fastening that held him, and fell down the ladder.

'He can't climb down,' said Mr Babbacombe. 'Only up. 'Tes a one-way world for all of us.' Robot got up and limped across to his master and leaned on him.

Mr Babbacombe stood up, and was taking short breaths. 'Listen,' he said.

They listened. There was the wind, and there was the moving of foliage. There was the sea not far distant. There was the rain falling and its fallen liquid running. There was nothing else.

There was something not heard but felt, a trembling underfoot. Then there was an unsticking noise, as if the sea had been lifted up in one clinging piece and dropped again. After it there was another shake and then a noise like the slow falling of a tree, once, twice, and a third time.

Sergeant Lowes would have gone to the door then and looked out. Mr Babbacombe put a hand on his arm. 'Wait,' he said.

There was a fourth falling crash, and something

121

plunged against the door of the building, pushing it hard against the wall, since it was an outside sliding door.

'That's all four,' said Mr Babbacombe. 'There's no more to signify. I hope you still have time to get up the cliff.'

Sergeant Lowes was at the door now, trying to pull it open. But whatever held it against the building would not release it.

'The dairy door,' said Jane. 'Go out through that.'

The dairy door was a small one at the side of the building. They went out of it and across the yard. Now, ahead of them, across the road, and up against the shippon, a tree seemed to have grown. But it had not grown there. It had fallen, and into the wind as well, from its place below the cliff. It filled the road, lying right across it and into the hedge of the field on the far side.

'Go through,' said Sergeant Lowes. 'Here, young man, take my torch. I'll go on ahead and get my car down to the bottom and put a bit of light on the scene from there.'

David handed the torch to Martin and told him to help Jane for a minute. He followed Sergeant Lowes and looked for his own car. It was unharmed. Five feet behind it lay the trunk of a tree, and ten feet in front lay another. It would not be possible to get it out to-night. He switched its headlamps on, to give more illumination, and went back to Jane and Martin.

The first tree was the worst one. David had plunged his way through it without thinking, and he was wet to begin with, so that the sodden foliage had damped him little more. But when he came back more deliberately to the task of making his way through he saw how truly difficult it is to clamber through the top of a tree that is lying on its side, with half its branches crushed and broken underfoot and others snapped overhead, and all in darkness but for a lamp carried by someone else.

The subsequent trees were somewhat easier, because with those they could go down to the trunk and clamber over that. There were four big trees down, and those were what they had heard. But many others had fallen too, as if a long line of ground had tipped on its side.

Jane was astride the third tree when it shifted again, settling on to its crown more firmly. They were all safely off it when it moved, more than settling, and rolled over towards them as if it had lost its treelike immobility and become possessed of locomotion.

They came through all the fallen trees and to a piece of ground that had become broken. The road had lifted, or fallen, or perhaps just moved to one side or another. Its hedge, to the field side, had fallen as if it had been ploughed, some one way some another. On the cliff side there was no land now, but a blackness with cruel straight edges, and a noise of water in it.

Ahead of them Sergeant Lowes was making hard going of it, in the dark. He had assumed that the ground would stay more or less as he had known it, but it had not. And as he lost the road underfoot he lost his destination too: the side lights of the car at the top of the cliff. They should have guided him to the region of the Swallows, which were just below the car. But when he looked for the white of the road he seemed to see only the cliff, and no road.

Then, with his eyes used to the night, he saw where he was: he was where he meant to be, between the two larger Swallows. They were gaping pits under the cliff, unreflecting, and silent no more. They were empty, and deep in them something roared.

15

Sergeant Lowes was still standing in the road when the others came up to him. The roaring in the Swallows was continuous, a loud low bubbling snarl, monstrous and menacing. The Sergeant was brought to a standstill by it, and stood listening in the rain.

David pushed him. 'Go on,' he shouted, and stood aside to hand on Jane and Martin and Mr Babbacombe.

Sergeant Lowes woke from his audience with the depth, stared at those who had come to him, and went on. Mr Babbacombe, and with him Robot, stopped. David stood too. He thought it would be useless to push Mr Babbacombe on at once; he would have to look and listen and possibly say something. He stood near, but watched the rest of the party.

They walked along the road, and then they came to the chasm, the trench that Mr Babbacombe had been filling for the last few days. It had widened again. It was the same split in the earth that had been alongside the road after they had come through the trees. Martin had the torch. David could hear them talking about the best way of crossing.

'Water, water rising,' shouted Sergeant Lowes, who

had shaken off his bemusement.

David could half distinguish the words and make out the meaning. He knew that the noise in the Swallows was water too, and he could hear it all round him, water everywhere above the ground and under it, and hardly a firmament between them, hardly a place to stand.

'I never saw this before,' said Mr Babbacombe. 'It was never come to this before. 'Tes the sea, come up again to take the land. But I can beat it yet; it shan't have all its winnings. Where's my gun, young man, that you took yesterday?'

'It's in my car,' said David. 'But it won't do anything about this; this is water.'

'Fool,' said Mr Babbacombe, 'as if I could think to fend that off with a gun. No, that's doom. But I'll have my gun before I go from here.'

He turned away and went back towards the farm. David looked to see what the other party was doing. He found them getting across the trench. Sergeant Lowes was across, and Martin could skip back and forth easily. Jane was hesitating. David came to her.

'I'm not frightened,' she said. 'I know I shall fall in, that's all. I can't jump so far.'

David drew her back several yards, put his arm round her waist, held a resisting hand, and ran her to the brink, into the air, and on to the further edge. They did not land very well: David was fairly on the edge, but it gave beneath him, and Jane came against it with her shins and cried out. Sergeant Lowes and Martin pulled at them until they were up and away from the edge.

'Where's Dad?' said Jane, through tears of pain.

'Gone back for his gun,' said David. 'He doesn't want to come without it.'

'Why not?' said Jane. 'He doesn't value it. He's tried

125

to sell it, but it's worth nothing. I don't think he wants to come away from the farm.'

'One of us goes back for him,' said Sergeant Lowes. 'I think it'd better be you, young man. I'll be more use at the car. But have a care.'

'Give me the lamp,' said David.

They watched him leap the gap. 'They'd better be prompt,' said Sergeant Lowes. 'Or we'd better look for some long woods to make a bridge. I think we'll go up to the car first and send a message back, and if necessary we'll put the car in the gap and let them climb across it.'

Martin was not sure why anyone had gone back at all. He thought that the idea of putting the car across the gap was the most dramatic instance for some time. He felt that any element of adventure in what they were doing now was spoilt by the wet and the dark and the anti-climax of life continuing after its end.

They walked up the road to the top of the cliff. Sergeant Lowes felt a spasm of tightened muscle across his back, and saw that he would be fit only for bed in the morning. Jane felt her heart tighten for the double perils of two people she was bound to, down there in the dark.

There was someone near David's car. She did not know who it was. Then she saw Robot with him, and knew it was her father. She heard Robot bark, still excited. Mr Babbacombe and Robot crossed the yard, distinct in light from the house door and the shippon and the yard light. They darkened the doorway and went in. At the edge of the yard, half obscured by the fallen tree, glimmered the lamp David had.

Sergeant Lowes was in the car, wiping his hands and face dry and speaking over the radio to Marret.

Light showed on his face. Near him, but not in the car yet, stood Martin.

Jane heard three things. To her right there was a new noise on the cliff, of something moving and stretching, and of chalk falling. From the house below came the barking of Robot, then a gunshot, and no more barking.

The glimmer of light at the edge of the yard broke through the tree and began to move quickly. But it was not far on its way when there was another gunshot. The light in the kitchen went out, but the other lights stayed on. David, if that was the explanation of the smaller moving light, ran on to the house, and his lamplight vanished for a moment. It appeared again, and stood still for a long time. Those were the three sounds and the accompanying sights.

The fourth sound was heard by all on the cliff. The lights of the house flickered. There was a rumble and clatter, and then the light was greater, not just the shining out of windows, but the shining out of whole rooms: the side of the house had come away. Jane saw dust fly. Martin came to look with her, and Sergeant Lowes cut his message short and brought his aching back to the cliff edge again.

Then, in the light of its own internal self, they saw, and they heard, the house collapse, and its lights go out, and then the shippon lights, and it was all darkness down there but for the lamps of David's car, away in a separate place.

'I don't think we can do anything, my dear,' said Sergeant Lowes. 'Whatever he decided to do, it's either done or not needing to be done now, and I think we'd better take ourselves away now and let someone else do the looking.'

'Both of them,' said Jane. 'Both of them. Can I sit in your car?'

'Yes,' said Sergeant Lowes. 'That'd be best, and then when you feel like it we'll go back to Marret.'

Martin stayed out of the car for a time. It was not clear to him that anyone need be harmed, but then he had not seen them near the house, or heard the gun fired. He looked into the formless uncharted night. He heard the land moving below the cliff, sliding away from the cliff. He heard the waters rising to meet the waters falling out of the chalk.

He saw a light waken down there and begin to move among the fallen trees.

'They're there,' he shouted, not doubting that they were both together. The single light moved towards the car lamps and flashed them. Martin reported back. Sergeant Lowes started his car, angled it on the road so that it pointed down to the car below, and flashed his lamps.

'We'll go down,' he said. 'Get in, Martin.' Martin got in and they went down the cliff.

There was a place where they had to stop, either a yard short, still on the chalk, of the gap, where they could move again up the cliff; or the car could go into the gap and remain there, but become a bridge. Sergeant Lowes tried the radio, but he was in a radio black-out area down here, and could hear and send nothing. They sat and watched the water ahead of them under the headlights.

The trench was full of water now, and it was flowing out over the other edge and into the Swallows. The road between the Swallows was still above water, however.

'He'll have to look sharp,' said Sergeant Lowes.

'They will,' said Martin.

'There'll be only one,' said Sergeant Lowes. 'And we can't do much to help him; if he can't come by himself then another hand won't speed him.'

They waited. Jane began to sob, and there was nothing, Sergeant Lowes considered, that could possibly help. Martin was bored, and yawned. There was a thought that was due to come to him, he knew, and he could even sense what it was through the protective wrapping, but he did not want to think it yet, because it was half a glad thought and half a devastating one. So many things this year had been inexact, impossible to categorize as good or bad, enjoyable or sad. Thinking, perhaps, was becoming too much for his mind, sickening it instead of nourishing.

A walking, staggering figure came into the edge of the light fanning in front of the car. It came to the place between the Swallows, and there it stopped and looked at the waters that had filled them again.

The same swift rush that Martin had seen before came again. The water rose over the road, up the legs of the escaping walker, and then higher and higher, until he stood with his arms up, and the water stretched back towards the car and began to rise against the headlamps and slap under the footwells.

The water went down, as it had gone down before, into a whirlpool, and into the whirlpool went the walker. They saw him being taken round and round, held up as the water gyrated. Then the water went away out of sight, and no one was there. And they sat and watched while its level was restored again, and the Swallows lay calm and still and very full.

But that was only for a time. Another upwelling of water came from the trench in front of them, and the land beyond shifted, fast enough for Martin to feel that he had moved instead. Sergeant Lowes started to move the car backwards up the slope, and came backwards to the top of the cliff at last.

'We'd better be off,' he said. 'But I think we'll wait a moment for somebody to come out from Marret. I know that's a trial for you, Jane, but we weren't expecting anything sudden like this.'

'I'll get out,' said Jane. 'I feel choked and sick.'

'A little more wet won't harm you,' said Sergeant Lowes. He got out of the car himself, to take Jane's arm and keep her from the edge of the cliff.

'Best not go that way,' he said. 'There's nothing to see.'

'I must,' said Jane. Sergeant Lowes went with her, and they stood together on the road and looked out. The only object visible was David's car. Then that was obscured by something that moved in front of it. Jane had a sudden hope for a moment, but then the car's own lights showed that it was the head of a tree. Then the car moved, and she hoped again, knowing that the hope was useless and that a car could not be driven out of that place.

'Floating,' said Sergeant Lowes. 'Water under it.'

The car was floating. It swung round, lit for a moment a tumbled flood, and then faded, its lamps going out. Now there was nothing at all but the sound of water and the shifting of the ground.

'We'd best move right off the edge,' said Sergeant Lowes. 'We don't know how the ground lies beneath us.'

Jane let herself be led back to the car. They drove along the road, and waited at the end of it, by the gate at the main road, for whoever came from Marret.

A car came, and an ambulance. Martin and Jane were led to the ambulance, and the fresh car and Sergeant Lowes went back to the cliff top. The new crew had a searchlight with them, and with it they raked the scene below.

The farm was crumbling at the foot of the cliff. The water from the land had washed its way under it for centuries, and the sea had undermined from the other side. There was no strength in the join between the chalk and the lower land, and along here the water had hollowed a trench, and the farm had moved away from the mainland. It was now an island, and a crumbling island too. The sea was now eating its way along the edge of the chalk and pulling the farmland down. By itself, and its own weight, the farmland was settling lower and lower.

Sergeant Lowes left after some time and winced his way home, because his muscles were now tightened all down his back. The other two men stayed all night, reporting at intervals. There was nothing else they could do. By the light of morning they saw a group of crumbling islands in a stained brown sea, and towards the sunrise, where the current took it, a mass of floating trees and wood and bales of hay. Swallow Farm had gone down to the sea at last, as Black Babbacombe had expected.

16

'More like spasm between the shoulder blades,' said Sergeant Lowes. 'When I breathe.'

'Mine is lower down and to the sides,' said Constable Zeal. 'Still in the thoracic area, though.'

'Oh yes,' said Sergeant Lowes, understandingly, but secretly wondering whether Constable Zeal meant that his bottom ached, with that long word.

'Ribs, of course,' said Constable Zeal. Sergeant Lowes put his elbow on the pillow and edged himself a little higher up in bed. A sewing machine stitched its way across his shoulder, and somebody pulled the thread tight.

'You all right, Sergeant?' said Constable Zeal.

'Just moving,' said Sergeant Lowes, putting the telephone under his ear where it would lie without being held. There was a tumbling noise from the other end of the line. 'Hello,' said Sergeant Lowes. 'Are you all right?'

'Just let the handset drop,' said Constable Zeal, from his bed some streets away. 'Reaching across for the knitting needle. It's boots this time. Pink.'

'Oh yes,' said Sergeant Lowes. 'Well, I was telling you; there we were on this cliff, and I could feel my muscles ratching up. I always reckon it started up when I had a fall much the same as you and laid up a day or two. Every picture tells a story: you don't recover your full strength without you take extra care.'

'Yes,' said Constable Zeal. 'I've enough aching of my own, Sergeant, without your case-load. And now you've whetted my appetite with half a report, and you've gone back to your own aches again.'

Sergeant Lowes was silent for a while. 'Constable Zeal,' he said, but with less dignity than he wanted because of not being able to fill his lungs full of air without activating an extra set of muscular steel girders bolted in round him as he slept. 'Constable Zeal, I've a distinct impression that you are anticipating some future elevation of rank. In other words, I'm still your Sergeant, and you listen to me whatever I say, on or off duty, and when you're an Inspector I'll listen to you. I know I'll always be a Sergeant, and that's enough for me, and it entitles me to respect from Constables.'

There was a burble and a sort of senile giggle from the other end of the line. Cracked, thought Sergeant Lowes. And not just ribs. He hitched himself up again, because the more nearly he was sitting up the more satisfying the waiting belch would be.

'Sorry about that,' said the telephone. 'The baby got into the circuit; it's a terrible switchboard in our house.'

'Did you hear what I said, then?' said Sergeant Lowes. He recovered his belch, of black pudding, and immediately felt less affronted by Constable Zeal.

'No,' said Constable Zeal. 'You're still teetering on the edge of the cliff. New readers begin here, eh?'

'Well listen, then,' said Sergeant Lowes. 'I'm just telling it to you to get it straight in my mind before writing it out in a report. Anyway, you'll know where I was and what you can see from there.'

'Yes,' said Constable Zeal. 'Goodbye, chooky chooky choo, bye bye.' There were several distinct kisses.

'I don't know whether I ought to be listening to all this,' said Sergeant Lowes. 'It sounds highly compromising, like what you hear on a tapped telephone.'

'I've swapped the baby for a cup of tea,' said Constable Zeal. 'Warm, wet and rather sweet.'

'Let me go on with my story,' said Sergeant Lowes. 'Oh, no, wait a minute, here comes my cup of tea. Constable, I bet my girl's prettier than yours.'

'Unlikely,' said Constable Zeal. 'Beauty being in the eye of the beholder, and all that.'

'Ah,' said Sergeant Lowes, 'but I've got Jane Babbacombe.'

'If I were Inspector I'd relieve you of that duty,' said Constable Zeal. 'Sergeant.'

*　　*　　*

'You don't need to do anything,' Mrs Lowes had said. 'I mean, where else can you go?' So Jane and Martin had stood soaking in the little hallway of the house while she climbed the stairs like a bird up and down the side of its cage, had dried and warmed them both, briskly taken Martin's clothes and cleaned and pressed them, and sent them to bed. In the morning she had sent Martin off to school, 'for,' she said, 'he'll do no good loafing round the house all day and he has to go back sooner or later.' Then she had twittered to the headmaster of the school about Martin, and set

134

Jane to clear up the breakfast things. Now Jane was taking the Sergeant a cup of tea.

*   *   *

Martin had retained, as the most important part of the previous night, the fact of the ambulance ride into Marret, with its end not at a hospital but at a stranger's house. That was his most immediate personal experience, he thought.

Others, however, thought he should be more concerned with what had happened at Swallow Farm. '*Tell us, now,*' said Stinking Tom, getting him into the gym cupboard even before school began. 'We've *seen*, but we don't *know*.'

'Seen?' said Martin.

'That your *house* isn't *there*,' said Stinking Tom.

'*Gone*,' said Pewter, with particular emphasis.

'Yes,' said Martin. 'I know that. I came to Marret in an ambulance.'

'But what about *all* those *deaths*?' said Stinking Tom, with his usual delicate stresses.

'Oh, those,' said Martin, feeling a sort of dizziness as if they were matters in a world thousands of feet below him, on another plane perhaps that had no relationship truly of up or down or across with his, just nearness. 'They got washed away. There was a car washed away too,' he added. That was easier to think of and might distract Stinking Tom a little. But in the end it was the assembly bell that took them all to assembly. Stinking Tom smelt of toadstools, the rot on wood. Today, stink or not, he was part of Martin's shelter, and by standing in Martin's glory he kept the world off him, being an exclusive agent and a buffer.

In the afternoon, when school ended, he was called for by a Police Car, which came into the school grounds a little bit faster than the headmaster liked; he stopped Martin in the hall and told him to pass the message on, he was in too much of a hurry himself to do it.

Martin sat in the car and wondered why it had come. The driver said it was to take him to his sister, by order of Sergeant Lowes. Martin let things be as they were, and questioned nothing. He passed on no message about driving too fast in the school grounds.

The car went down to the harbour, merely a walking distance, in fact. Here there was Sergeant Lowes standing stiffly and pale. Here too was Jane, merely pale, dressed in a coat not her own. Sergeant Lowes waved the Police Car to stop some distance off, and then nodded to someone down on the water. Martin's driver got out and sent away two small boys who had begun to gather and constitute a crowd in the road at the end of the jetty.

*   *   *

'This may not be very pleasant for you, my dear,' said Sergeant Lowes, after he had the telephone call from the Station during the afternoon. He had got up and come downstairs, where Mrs Lowes brisked him up and pulled his tunic straight since he had not the lively muscles to do it himself.

'Nor you don't have to do it,' he added, between short bursts of the electric razor at his chin.

'But,' he added, 'you'd probably rather know for sure. You aren't a qualified witness for this, no more than I am. They rang up from the Station to say a

fishing boat was bringing in a man they found in the
sea. They didn't say much, for they didn't know, but
I reckon it's the young one. Now, that's the one you
can't identify, Jane, because you're not a relative, but
if you're willing to come to the harbour and look, then
I think we'd be glad of it. For all that, it may be some
stranger.'

'I should want to know,' said Jane.

'I don't reckon it's your Dad,' said Sergeant Lowes.
'Not at all.' He reckoned that the recovery of that body
would be better left until the general day of resurrec-
tion and not come casually, shattered as it must be by
gunshot. But he did not think that Jane would come
across these thoughts.

They went down to the harbour, and were there
before the fishing boat pulled to the jetty. She saw a
bundle wrapped in sailcloth, and looked and looked at
it. No one took any notice of it, and she wondered if it
could be a sail bagged in itself.

Martin came, in a Police Car, but stayed in the road.

'Can you manage the ladder?' said Sergeant Lowes.
'I think we got here a bit soon, or they'd have brought
him up on top. Do you think you can do it, ladder and
job?'

'Yes,' said Jane. She went down the ladder slippery
at the side of the jetty. Brown hands with scales caught
her and helped her to the bottom of the boat. The
scales were from the fish, she thought, not natural
growths. Sergeant Lowes was down next, and making
a worse trip of it than Jane, not being able so well to
accommodate to the up and down movement of the
boat and the lack of movement of the ladder.

'Let's hear about it,' he said to the fishermen. Jane
heard about seeing something pale in the water, and
pulling it inboard, and wrapping it in what they had.

The bundle she had seen was not what they were to look at. There was a smaller one at the front of the boat. A fisherman lifted a fold of tarpaulin and there was a pale face.

'David,' said Jane, and the sun set, twilight came over the harbour and the town sank lightless. But she held to a halyard and only bowed her head a little. The evening fall of the dew of sweat passed over her skin, her head ached, and she saw again. 'David,' she said again.

The fisherman was saying that they had done what they knew, artificial respiration, but it had been no use. They had then had to put him aside, as he was, and come in, sending a message on ahead with a faster boat.

'Thank you,' said Sergeant Lowes. 'Cover him up, lad.'

David opened his eyes, unseeingly, moved, and vomited a great quantity of water.

A fisherman said he was an artful bugger, laying there and letting them work at him like that.

'You let him be,' said Sergeant Lowes. 'He had a busy night.'

Jane went up the ladder. Sergeant Lowes would have followed her, but the gap between boat and ladder was too much for him, though he was willing. Jane understood what to do, however, and went to the Police Car and handed on instructions anyone would assume Sergeant Lowes to have given. When the ambulance came, and first David had been swung up from the boat, and then the Sergeant, she went with them both to the hospital. David was put to bed. Sergeant Lowes was massaged and sent home.

*   *   *

He was such a nice young man,' said Miss Slingsby, at about the moment David was being sick. 'I had quite an affection for him, and many's the good laugh we had together, Mr Dawson.'

'Really?' said Mr Dawson. 'I never credited him with any sense of humour, Miss Slingsby. Personable and pleasant, yes, knowledgeable in his work even assiduous. However, we could do a lot worse with the next one they send us, Miss Slingsby. How they come and go, over the years. Have you ever thought what a small world we live in, Miss Slingsby? I don't mean in the way that we keep meeting people we know, or who know our friends, but that we don't go very far to meet other people. We like to live in our own little world. All I want to know about other people is what is in those files there. Otherwise I'm quite happy to walk from here to my house tonight, and back here in the morning, and really, not meet any new people. Even my wife, you know, I've known all my life. She tells me that I met her in this very room, at a party. I was about eight at the time, and the doctor's children had a birthday. I can remember sitting on the floor in front of that cupboard, well, it was a cupboard then, and turning round and there was a little girl looking at me so admiringly and pulling her hair ribbon out in her admiration. And I selfishly wouldn't put down the model aeroplane I was playing with and attend to her. And here we are now, married all these years. How strange is the turn of the world, Miss Slingsby. Now may I help you on with your coat?'

'Yes, indeed,' said Miss Slingsby. 'What a romantic story, Mr Dawson. Are you sure your wife remembers?'

'Yes indeed,' said Mr Dawson. 'Remembered it long after we were married, when we were recalling how this was the director's house. She didn't know it was me, though, after all those years, and I remembered too, not knowing it had been her. Good night, Miss Slingsby. It is a sad day for us.'

'Yes indeed,' said Miss Slingsby.

* * *

The body of Black Babbacombe was never found. David was able to remember a scene in the farmhouse, which he described to Sergeant Lowes but added to the list of things he had forgotten when Jane asked him. His real forgetting started when the water was at waist level and he knew he was dead. As far as he knew he remained dead until he was in hospital, but there were long dreams of swimming in the dark, and floating. Now they live in Barchester, and Martin is still at school there. His niece starts next year, and Martin David Hayman in two years' time.

Miss Slingsby keeps wondering about Mr Dawson. Can it be true? She has not mentioned the matter again to Mr Hayman or to Mr Dawson. Mr and Mrs Hayman are both sure when they first met.